"I'll have you know that I have never, ever done this…this…stuff with anyone before."

"You mean *this* stuff?" Turning her around, and pressing her back into the flour sacks, Hunt consumed Carolina's mouth and, once again, she was lost in sensation.

Her head dropped back on her shoulders and when he finally released her, she exhaled a groan of disgust with herself. "Yes, *that* stuff."

What on earth had just happened? Hunt wondered. Had to be tension. Yeah. That was it. What else could have possessed him to kiss Carolina Brubaker of all people? He glanced at her and wondered what was going on in her head.

She was standing there, gaping into a compact, applying fresh lipstick. Cool as a cucumber all right.

And here he was, panting like a blasted bull eyeing the swirling red cape.

Dear Reader,

From a Texas sweetheart to a Chicago advice columnist, our heroines will sweep you along on their journeys to happily ever after. Don't miss the tender excitement of Silhouette Romance's modern-day fairy tales!

In *Carolina's Gone A' Courting* (SR #1734), Carolina Brubaker is on a crash course with destiny—and the man of her dreams—*if* she can survive their summer of forced togetherness! Will she lasso the heart of her ambitious rancher? Find out in the next story in Carolyn Zane's THE BRUBAKER BRIDES miniseries.

To this once-burned plain Jane a worldly, sophisticated, handsome lawyer is *not* the kind of man she wants…but her heart has other plans. Be there for the transformation of this no-nonsense woman into the beauty she was meant to be, in *My Fair Maggy* (SR #1735) by Sharon De Vita.

Catch the next installment of Cathie Linz's miniseries MEN OF HONOR, *The Marine Meets His Match* (SR #1736). His favorite independent lady has agreed to play fiancée for this military man who can't resist telling her what to do. If only he could order her to *really* fall in love.…

Karen Rose Smith brings us another emotional tale of love and family with *Once Upon a Baby…* (SR #1737). This love-leery sheriff knows he should stay far away from his pretty and pregnant neighbor—he's not the husband and father type. But delivering her baby changes everything.…

I hope you enjoy every page of this month's heartwarming lineup!

Mavis C. Allen
Associate Senior Editor

Please address questions and book requests to:
Silhouette Reader Service
U.S.: 3010 Walden Ave., P.O. Box 1325, Buffalo, NY 14269
Canadian: P.O. Box 609, Fort Erie, Ont. L2A 5X3

Carolina's Gone A'Courting

CAROLYN ZANE

THE BRUBAKER BRIDES

SILHOUETTE *Romance*®

Published by Silhouette Books

America's Publisher of Contemporary Romance

For Wendy Warren. Beautiful wife, loving mother, hilarious, loyal, encouraging friend, award-winning writer, fellow hypochondriac, all around wonder-woman and some day—twenty-one years, give or take—the mother-in-law to my son…if we should live that long, oy.

1 John 4:12

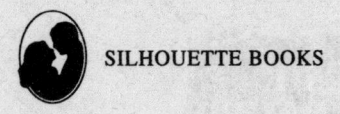 SILHOUETTE BOOKS

ISBN 0-373-19734-9

CAROLINA'S GONE A'COURTING

Copyright © 2004 by Carolyn Suzanne Pizzuti

Visit Silhouette Books at www.eHarlequin.com

Printed in U.S.A.

CAROLYN ZANE

lives with her husband, Matt, and their three children in the rolling countryside near Portland, Oregon's Willamette River. Like Chevy Chase's character in the movie *Funny Farm*, Carolyn finally decided to trade in a decade of city dwelling and producing local television commercials for the quaint country life of a novelist. And, even though they have bitten off decidedly more than they can chew in the remodeling of their hundred-plus-year-old farmhouse, life is somewhat saner for her than for poor Chevy. The neighbors are friendly, the mail carrier actually stops at the box and the dog, Bob Barker, sticks close to home.

THE BRUBAKER FAMILY TREE

Tiny Brubaker m. Miss Bernice

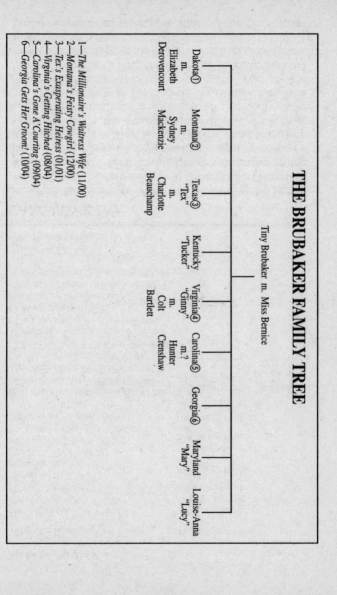

Dakota① m. Elizabeth Derovencourt

Montana② m. Sydney Mackenzie

Texas③ "Tex" m. Charlotte Beauchamp

Kentucky "Tucker"

Virginia④ "Ginny" m. Colt Bartlett

Carolina⑤ m.? Hunter Crenshaw

Georgia⑥

Maryland "Mary"

Louise-Anna "Lucy"

1—*The Millionaire's Waitress Wife* (11/00)
2—*Montana's Feisty Cowgirl* (12/00)
3—*Tex's Exasperating Heiress* (01/01)
4—*Virginia's Getting Hitched* (08/04)
5—*Carolina's Gone A 'Courting* (09/04)
6—*Georgia Gets Her Groom!* (10/04)

Chapter One

When Hunter Crenshaw agreed to help his uncle Mike drive horse-drawn carriages for the Hidden Valley Rodeo Days Fourth of July celebration, he had no idea that there would be more fireworks in his buggy than there were in the sky.

As usual, the annual rodeo was a madhouse. Drawing people from all over the country, the four-day festivities swelled the normally sleepy Texas town to ten times its size. Traffic from Main Street to the fairgrounds was a weeklong nightmare, requiring a network of horses and buggies and taxicabs to ferry families from the overflow parking lot, down by Ned's Lonestar Grill, to the fairgrounds across town. Since this evening's rodeo was nearly over, the mad rush out of town was just beginning.

As he perched atop the wooden driver's seat of his old-fashioned rig, Hunt leaned forward, elbows to knees, reins dangling, and concentrated on Old Blue's broad behind in an attempt to shut out the embarrassing fracas in the back seat. The rhythmic swish of the old sorrel's tail, the clip clop of the iron shoes against concrete, the lanes of traffic easing through the town's handful of intersections—though distracting—did little to drown out the bickering.

"…or what it is you are driving at, Brandon. All evening I've been getting the impression that you are avoid—"

"Carolina, I'm not avoid—"

"—ing the real issue."

"—ing the real issue. I'm simply trying to find the words—"

The light ahead turned yellow. Then red.

"Whoa, now, Blue." Hunt gave the reins a gentle tug and settled in to watch the traffic ooze through the intersection. He rotated his head and shoulders to ease the tension of sitting in the same position for hours on end. That, and listening to Miss "Buck's Up" Brubaker and her idiotic boyfriend, Brandon McGraw, verbally duke it out.

"—as if I'm some kind of Dresden doll."

"Believe me when I say I don't think of you as a Dresden—"

"Then just tell me what is making you so…"

Freaking miserable? Hunt wondered in disgust. The woman was giving him a splitting headache. He could only imagine what the poor slob behind him must be suffering.

"…would tell you if you'd simply *listen* to—"

"It's as if I'm going to…to…*bite* you for heaven's sake!"

Hunt cocked his head. Across town, the post-rodeo fireworks show had started. Drums pounded. Tubas squeaked. Trumpets and flutes struck the usual number of discordant notes, but it mattered not on this particular day of the year. The national anthem swelled from the center of the arena, and the fair-to-bursting crowd's boisterous cheers could certainly be heard all the way to the satellite that twinkled down from its orbit in space.

As, no doubt, could the argument in the back seat.

"A…time-out? Just what do you mean, by—" Carolina Brubaker's voice grew sarcastic "—'time-out'? We are not in grade school, Brandon."

"I know. I mean that I think things are moving a little bit too fast, and I…I…I…need some time to…to…to *think,* that's all."

"Think? That's what this is all about? I can certainly give you time to think, if that's all you need."

"I…I…you…you…I…I…"

Jaws jumping, Hunt gave his gum a vicious once-over and fought the urge to turn around and straighten out their petty differences. But he didn't. He was working for Uncle Mike tonight. And lecturing the patrons was hardly good for business. Especially considering that the spidery gold lettering on the side of the carriage boasted:

Crenshaw's Romantic Moonlight Carriage Rides. Call and reserve us for your prom, engagement, wedding and special occasion needs today."

"I don't understand, Brandon. Please, just spit it out—"

"Okay." Brandon drew a deep breath. "I think I'm in love with your sister."

Hunt's brow rocketed up under the brim of his Stetson.

"All of this—" her voice was fraught with frustration "—this 'time-out' psychobabble is really—"

"Georgia. Your younger sister, Georgia. I think I'm in love with Georgia."

"—getting on my nerves. Clearly, we've been spending too much time double-dating with my sister Ginny and her husband. God love her, but because she's a psychologist, she does tend to blather about all that psychological cr—"

"—and I'm thinking about asking her to go out with me."

"—ap, and I think we—"

Hunt snorted and flicked his hat back on his head with his thumb.

The light changed and the argument escalated.

"—simply need to relax, that's all. For heaven's sake, Brandon."

"And I plan on telling Georgia my feelings as soon—"

Carolina's voice grew wary. Slow. *"Georgia?"* She paused and Hunt could feel the little hairs at his nape stand at attention.

The grand finale of the fireworks show suddenly burst forth in a profusion of color against the velvety blackness of the night sky. Hunt watched the beauty unfurl overhead as, behind him, Pandora's box unfurled.

In Hunt's humble opinion, this Brandon character was probably doing the first smart thing he'd done since meeting this woman; cutting his losses and bailing out now. Yep. Carolina Brubaker was just another spoiled rich girl.

And he oughta know.

During the day, Hunt worked as a ranch hand for Big Daddy Brubaker, billionaire oil tycoon and owner of the immense Circle BO ranch, just outside of Hidden Valley. And in his years working there, he'd seen his share of bratty debutantes. In fact, Hunt had run into Carolina on more than one occasion this summer, since she and her sisters had come to visit their uncle and aunt. She'd never given him the time of day, though he'd saddled her mount for her on more than one occasion. She'd flounce into the stable with her friends, chattering a mile a minute, not sparing him so much as a glance or a how-do-you-do. And tonight, she hadn't seemed to recognize him at all as he'd helped her into the carriage.

He smirked.

Though he didn't know her well, he'd formed his opinions. Made his judgments. And, guessing from the tears and histrionics going on behind him, she was a regular hellcat. For crying in the night, people were beginning to stare. Although, as much as he hated to admit it, she did have a bit of a case. Having your boyfriend dump you for your sister had to smart.

"My *sister?*" Carolina shrieked. "*You have fallen in love* with my…*sister?*" She jumped to her feet, rocking the carriage, and smashed Brandon over the head with her red-white-and-blue souvenir rodeo pompom.

Yep. Hunt cringed. Folks were hanging out of their car windows. Stopping on the sidewalk. Gaping at the fools in his carriage. This had to be bad for business. He turned around. "Uh, excuse me there, but—" He donned his customer-relations smile and was about to— as diplomatically as possible—ask them to shut up, but Carolina was on a roll. A roll fueled by hurt and embarrassment and righteous indignation.

"You can't fall in love with my sister! Why, that's just…just *creepy!*"

Turning back around, Hunt squinted off beyond the traffic and pondered her accusation. No, not creepy. Stupid as all get-out, yes, but only creepy if this Georgia gal was *Brandon's* sister.

"It wasn't creepy when I was dating your older sister, Ginny, and you wanted to go out with *me*."

Hunt's jaw went slack and he darted another glance over his shoulder. This guy really was an idiot.

"But that was different! You didn't love Ginny."

"Exactly," Brandon reasoned.

Carolina gasped as several dreadful realizations dawned.

Hunt urged Old Blue forward, and Carolina dropped back into her seat with a thud. From there, the argument began a death spiral and, finally reaching his boiling point, Brandon tapped Hunt on the shoulder and demanded that they stop at once.

"No problem." Hunt shrugged. It wasn't as if they were going much past a mile or two per hour, anyway.

Brandon gripped the buggy's handrails and, catapulting himself into the oncoming traffic, signaled a cab headed in the opposite direction.

"Brandon! Wait!" Carolina's shrill voice rose above the idling engines. "I'm not finished *talking* to you!" When Brandon opened the cab's door, she fired the rest of her rodeo souvenirs at his backside.

Brandon shook off the cotton candy and Beanie Baby horses and jumped into the cab. "Good night, Carolina. We'll talk when you are not so irrational." The slam of his door echoed in the wake of the sudden silence following the Hidden Valley High School marching band's final notes.

As he watched Brandon's taxi disappear onto a side street, Hunt felt a tiny fist flailing at his arm.

"Follow that cab!" Swinging her long legs up over the iron-and-wood seat back, Carolina leaped up onto the seat beside him and gesticulated at the taxi's disappearing taillights.

Hunt stared at her and then out at the ever-growing gridlock. "Are you kidding?"

"No!" She grabbed his driving crop and flicked Old Blue's broad rump. Startled, the horse began to trot. Past the bus and into the bike lane they rolled.

"Hey! Give me that!" Hunt grabbed Carolina's slender wrist and reached for the crop, but to no avail. She was a woman on a mission. And she was a helluva lot stronger than she looked. Like a blond banshee, she wailed after Brandon, her long hair wild, her cheeks molten, her eyes shooting sparks of rage. The woman was nuts. Certifiable.

Wacko.

They grappled and Carolina managed to get in another good sting. Old Blue's ears went flat in surprise. The couple fell back against the seat as the horse picked up momentum and jerked them toward a handicapped ramp that led to the sidewalk.

"Ho-now, Blue!" Hunt tried to calm the prancing animal and at the same time control the kook that had elbowed her way onto the driver's bench. "Whoa!" he shouted at the horse and then to Carolina, "Lady, would you please return to your seat!"

"Brandon!" Carolina snapped the crop in the air, *"Wait! I want to talk to you! You can't just drop a bomb on me and run away!"*

The passenger side wheels of the carriage mounted the curb and tossed Carolina across Hunt's lap. They narrowly missed a fire hydrant. When Carolina attempted to sit up, their heads collided. Hunt bit his lip and tasted blood. Ears twitching, nerves and rigging jangling, tail lifted, Old Blue left a pile of steaming horse apples in front of the Bender Shoe Emporium as he tried to obey his driver's crazed signals.

"Lady, I'm warning you—"

"Brandon!" Carolina tugged on the left rein and slapped the horse. *"You can't do this to me!"*

Poor Old Blue took her shouts to mean "giddy-up" and rumbled back off the sidewalk and into the oncoming traffic. Horns blared and Old Blue lumbered across the street without regard for the lights or oncoming traffic. He took a speed bump and they were airborne for what seemed to Hunt like a lifetime.

"Brandon! Get back heeeeeeere!"

Over the opposite curb they flew, sending rodeo revelers scattering as they clattered down the sidewalk. Old Blue dodged and wove in a skittish dance, sideswiping parked cars, ruining Independence Day decorations and crushing a display of shrubs that spelled out the words Home of the Free in the center of town square. Pigeons flapped in alarm as the carriage careened through the small park and gouged a deep and unforgivable scar into the bronze statue of Roy "Rusty" Harper, town founder.

By now they'd attracted the attention of a police officer who—sirens wailing—began pursuit. For fifteen hair-raising minutes they led the law on a low-speed chase down the sidewalk that caused a number of fender dents among rubber-neckers in the street.

Finally the police bullhorn demanded that they *"Stop! In the name of the law!"*

Unfortunately that was impossible, though Hunt would have gladly complied if he could have only pried the screaming Carolina off his neck. With the sickening scraping of wood on metal and metal on concrete, Old Blue cut too close to a parking meter, neatly severing his connection to the carriage. Nostrils filled with newfound freedom, Old Blue galloped off into the sunset.

Now under its own volition, the carriage veered off the sidewalk, through a picket fence, over a tidy scrap of lawn and into the widow Foster's front porch, destroying her garden and its flag-bearing gnomes and flamingos in the process. Hunt and Carolina landed badly on the porch, plunging through the widow's screen door and rolling into her entryway.

* * *

Carolina Brubaker had never been so mortified in her life.

First, Brandon's heinous defection and now…

This.

Somehow she'd managed to land atop the detestable Hunter Crenshaw in the entryway of some elderly woman's house. She blinked as a crocheted doily slipped off a table and draped over her face. Through the spidery webbing, Carolina could see the poor old dear clucking and flapping about as if she'd just spotted a drunk at a revival meeting.

"Land sakes, whatever are you doing? Here, now! This is a private residence and you are frightening my cats!"

Carolina frowned and, when she had the strength to suck in some of the wind that had been knocked from her lungs, pulled her head from Hunt's chest, shook off the doily and peered into his eyes.

It was then she knew she'd never forget the unmitigated rage that snapped there. *Dang it all.* Out of all the carriage drivers out on the road that night, he *would* have to work as a hand on her uncle's ranch. And, out of all the hands on her uncle's ranch, it *would* have to be Hunt.

Carolina had always avoided him, knowing he'd pigeonholed her years ago as a spoiled brat. Useless. Dumb. Blond. Even though he didn't know her from Eve. She'd always resented his arrogant attitude.

And so, she'd paid him back tit for tat.

He didn't speak to her; she didn't speak to him. He didn't acknowledge her existence; she didn't acknowledge his. He ignored her; she ignored him.

Too bad she couldn't ignore him now. Nope. Not while she floundered about on top of his rock-hard chest. Carolina sighed at the cruel fates that had her squirming as she attempted to disentangle her legs from his.

"Freeze, suckers!" The command blared from an electronic bullhorn in the doorway.

They froze.

The wounded screen door slammed shut and hard-soled footsteps tapped rapidly across the wooden floor. *"Widow Foster—"* the voice was still alarmingly amplified *"—are you all right?"*

A flustered voice answered, "I believe so, officer. Please, don't shoot them in my house."

Shoot?

Carolina licked her dry lips, buried her face in Hunt's neck and tightened her straddle on his hips. As she lay there whimpering, her heart slammed against his and her lungs inhaled his labored breath. For what seemed ages, his five-o'clock shadow abraded her nose as he angrily worked his gum. When Hunt ventured a slow-motion peek over her shoulder, his bravery and her own curiosity emboldened her to join him in this foray.

A stoop-shouldered, horn-rimmed, somewhat shaggy-haired officer of the law glared at them from behind a brass badge. The brief glimpse she caught did not tell Carolina if the officer was male or female, as the uniform and sturdy black police-issued shoes offered no clue. Neither did the hairless, nondescript face, nor the asexual, pear-shaped body type. Even the voice hovered somewhere between an alto and a tenor as the familiar words forcefully boomed through the bullhorn.

"You have the right to remain silent!"

Hunt's head thudded back to the floor.

Carolina ducked down and filled her fists with his shirt.

"Anything you say can be used against you in a court of law!"

"Oh, for crying out loud, Scruggs," Hunt snapped. "Its not like we planned this fiasco."

Scruggs? Carolina frowned. Still no clue.

"You have the right to have an attorney present now and during any further questioning—"

"C'mon, Scruggs. Don't do this."

"Quiet, Crenshaw. I haven't finished reading you your rights."

"What rights? I didn't do anything wrong! If you want to arrest someone—" Hunt gripped Carolina by the arms and thrust her into the air and held her out at Scruggs "—arrest her! She's a menace to society!"

Carolina gasped, her hair dangling into his face. How dare he? "How *dare* you?"

Hunt blew several blond locks away from his mouth. "Oh, come on, lady. You know perfectly well that none of this would have happened if you hadn't literally scared the crap out of my poor horse."

"I beg your pardon! If you had simply done as I asked—"

He gave her a little shake. "Hell's bells, woman! Do you ever listen to anyone without steamrolling over them with those blasted flapping lips?"

It was very hard to argue a point with him holding her as if she were a boneless rag doll. Carolina inhaled so deeply her nose snapped shut. "You…" she huffed. "You have *no right* to talk to me in such—"

"Oh, get off your snooty high horse and tell old Dragnet there the truth." He arched up and brought his nose to hers. "If it wasn't for you—"

"Quiiii-ette!" The bullhorn emitted some squeaky feedback that had the widow's cats yowling and scrambling. *"If you cannot afford an attorney, one will be appointed to you free of charge if you wish."*

"Aw, Scruggs, that's just plain insulting. Are you ever gonna get over grade school?"

"Not as long as you keep calling me Dragnet, Buster!"

Hunt sighed and dropped Carolina back down upon his chest. He cupped her face, none too gently. "Can you afford an attorney?"

She struggled to sit up, but he held her face captive, her lips squished between his thumb and forefinger like a puckered fish. "Yesh."

"Okay, then. We're fine, Scruggs. Now, turn that stupid thing off and let's all go home. I'm beat. We can sort all this out in the morning."

"Freeze, scum bucket!"

Again they froze. Even the widow stood stock-still. Hunt groaned.

"All right, then." Scruggs flicked off the bullhorn and, fishing a notebook from a hip pocket, began to scribble. "You are both under arrest for—"

"Arrest?" Hunt protested.

"What?" Legs flailing, eyes blazing, Carolina scrambled to her feet. She raked the disheveled haystack she'd so carefully coiffed for her date that evening over her shoulder and pointed at Scruggs. "Listen here! You can't arrest me! I have not done anything wrong. It is *his* fault…that…"

Officer Scruggs's eyes took a slow journey from Carolina's Italian leather cowboy boots, over her snug designer jeans, traveling the dips and swells of her western-style shirt and then landed most disconcertingly on her face. What was going on behind that owlish gaze?

Nonplussed, Carolina fell silent.

With a cocky flourish, Scruggs resumed scribbling. "You are both under arrest for the following charges— littering, evading an officer of the law, resisting arrest, failure to stop at numerous red lights, driving down the wrong side of the street, reckless endangerment and defacement of public and private property." Scruggs paused. "I'm sure there is more, but we can deal with that when we get you checked in down at the Gray Bar Hotel."

Hunt snorted and dragged himself to his feet.

"Listen, Scruggs. I don't have time for this baloney. How about I give your family a free pass for a carriage ride anytime you want and we'll call it good."

Scruggs grabbed a pen and murmured, "Bribery," then squinted at Hunt. "Anything else you want me to add?"

Carolina could feel Hunt's eyes shooting daggers at her back as he stooped to snatch his Stetson off the widow's floor. Giving it an angry smack against his thigh, he jammed it on his head and said, "Guess not."

"Ten-four. I'm holding the perps in the back seat, and I'll roll prints as soon as we get there, over." Scruggs set the radio down and slapped a flashing Kojak onto the roof of the squad car. A moment later, sirens began to wail.

Hunt groaned. They were sunk. Clearly, Eustace "Dragnet" Scruggs, Jr., still had it in for him. Ever since they'd been in the first grade, Eustace had fancied himself to be the "Dan Tana" of Hidden Valley Grade School. Couldn't blow your blasted nose without old Eustace tattling. Hunt had put up with the goofy lingo, the makeshift uniforms and weapons, not to mention the constant shadow lurking behind every corner until one day, when they were in sixth grade, Eustace had flopped his hairy toe over the line.

When Hunt had finally cornered Mary Helen Rogers for a blissful first kiss under the mistletoe, he'd been so high he'd feared he'd drop his harp through a cloud. Until, that is, old Eustace had summoned the law in the form of their teacher, Mrs. Eggleston, a hawk-nosed, whisker-chinned crone who'd marched him and Mary

Helen—their ears in the grip of her unrelenting claws—
to the principal's office.

Didn't find out till later that Eustace had been sweet
on Mary Helen. And thus the rivalry—lopsided though
it was—began. Eustace never forgave Hunt for his natural way with the girls, and Hunt couldn't seem to get
over Eustace's weirdness.

So Hunt had taunted. And Eustace had retaliated.

Hunt had spent many an afternoon in detention because of old Dragnet Scruggs. And here he was again.
Being driven to the principal's office. After all these
years. Handcuffed to bimbo Brubaker, to add insult to
injury. Hidden Valley's answer to Joan Collins. Vi-
ciously he attacked his gum, popping and cracking, attempting to give vent to his mounting frustration.

"Would you please refrain from snapping your
gum?" Carolina said, glaring at him.

"Why?"

"It's driving me bats."

"We can't have you going *crazy,* now, can we?" he
jeered. Grinding his teeth together, his gum let off a series of machine-gun-style pops. He grinned at her, but
knew it didn't reach his eyes.

"I don't know why you're being such a jerk." She
sniffed. "It's not my fault that the bullhorn freaked out
your horse."

"Listen, lady, my horse was freaked out long before
Dragnet caught up with us."

Carolina's expression became pinched, and she lowered her voice. "Will you stop insulting the officer?
You are only going to get us deeper into trouble."

"I have nothing to do with the trouble we're in. My
uncle Mike lost untold business because of your lunacy. Not to mention the damage to his carriage and the
horse that is only who knows where."

"What kind of a ranch hand can't control one silly horse?"

Hunt's head snapped around and he stared at her. *Aha!* So she *had* known he was a hand on her uncle's ranch. Yet, until this very minute, she hadn't acknowledged any acquaintance.

The little witch.

Using the hand that was cuffed to hers, he adjusted his hat over his eyes so that he wouldn't have to look at her smug expression. Her wrist dangled alongside his until she jerked it back into her lap. Incensed Hunt yanked their arms back into his lap. They scuffled, pushing and shoving and muttering insults until Eustace picked up his bullhorn.

"Knock it off, back there!"

"You're going to be sorry you ever got into my carriage tonight, lady."

"Ooo, I'm running scared now." She gave her head a defiant toss. "When my uncle hears about this, he'll fire you."

"Yeah, well when my uncle hears about this, he'll sue you."

Chapter Two

They sped across town in relative silence, save for the wail of the siren and Scruggs's occasional bullhorn orders for the exiting rodeo masses to *"Stand aside and let the law through."* Carolina hung her head and prayed that no one would recognize her as she crouched behind the officer like some kind of caged animal. The too-tight seat belt smashed her poor bustline flat and, because Hunt's hand was cuffed to hers, there was no way to adjust the problem without far too much…intimacy.

Then there was the matter of her aching legs. Even though her muscles screamed for relief, she had no choice but to hold her feet aloft until they reached the station. Certainly, she couldn't lean her legs against Hunt, and there was no way she'd let her priceless boots touch this revolting excuse for a squad car.

To call the passenger area of Officer Scruggs's vehicle a pigsty would be an insult to pigs everywhere. The dim light of the passing streetlamps revealed a landfill comprised of black, greasy banana peels, shrunken and molding apple cores, fetid bits of pizza and fossilized pucks that were at one time Ding-Dongs. On the floor in the corner between Carolina and her door, there was a pile of shredded paper that reminded her of the stuff her childhood hamster had used to build his nest. She only hoped the raisins that were scattered about on the seat were indeed raisins. She could feel rather than see Hunt's amused smirk as she scooted closer to him and away from the suspicious debris.

Fine. Let him laugh at her. She didn't care. About anything. Or—a lump surged into her throat—anyone.

He turned away, presenting her with his shoulder.

Filled with abject misery, she stared at the toes of her brand-new boots and thought of happier times. Times such as that very afternoon, when she'd spotted these beautiful boots in a department store window. Handmade, imported boots she'd purchased just for the rodeo. When she'd tried them on, with a skippy little two-step in front of the store mirror, she'd never dreamed her fantasy date with the dreamy Brandon would have ended here.

Humiliated beyond belief and under arrest.

Handcuffed to Hunter Crenshaw, no less.

She'd never been so wretched in her life. She glanced at Hunt's profile as he stared out the passenger window. The tiny muscle under his ear was working, and the veins stood out on his neck. A scalding flush tingled in her cheeks. He was mad. Carolina looked away. Really mad. The anger fairly radiated down his arm, making the metal of their handcuffs seem to buzz. In retrospect she guessed she couldn't blame him. But she'd been in shock. Brandon claimed he loved her *sister,* for crying out loud. Her favorite sister. Beautiful, kind, loving, sweet and generous Georgia. Did—she gnawed her lip, barely daring to contemplate the terrible thought—did Georgia love Brandon, too? Her eyes narrowed.

She'd kill her.

Later.

After she'd made bail.

With a heavy sigh she dropped her head against the seat, and her eyes slid shut. A tiny groan gurgled forth as she remembered the matter of her father and Big Daddy. When they found out that she'd been arrested on all those charges...

Carolina tried to swallow, but the muscles in her throat felt swollen shut, as if she'd been guzzling superglue. How, in a matter of mere minutes, had her entire universe shifted on its axis? Everyone, it seemed, was against her. What had she done to deserve this? She was a perfectly nice person. Not some hardened criminal. The back of her throat burned and her eyes suddenly felt too big for their sockets. But she would not cry. Not in front of Hunt.

For some reason the man infuriated her on levels she usually reserved for the politically insane. Maybe it was because he'd never even given her a chance before he'd passed judgment. Made up his mind that she was just another rich girl with no brains or morals. She sniffed. Whatever. If that's what he wanted to believe, then that was his problem. She had enough problems of her own.

Finally street signs indicating their destination loomed ahead. Officer Scruggs—evidently having studied at the Dukes of Hazard driving school—brodied into the police station's parking lot on what felt to Carolina like two wheels. With an inadvertent squeal of alarm she clutched Hunt's arm.

The squad car's interior filled with the aroma of burning rubber and roiling garbage as they came to a screeching halt in front of the police station's main door. Lights still flashing, Scruggs emerged from the squad car and opened the back door for the prisoners. Carolina made sure her smile was extrawide as she accepted the officer's assistance out of the back seat.

"Thank you, very much, s-s…" A tiny frown marred her brow. *Sir? Ma'am?* She still wasn't sure. "S-sweetheart," she finished lamely, figuring the sooner she made friends with the local law, the sooner she could go home and take a shower.

Hunt emitted a strangled sound.

Scruggs seemed to take a bit of a shine to her friendly demeanor. "Pardon the mess there, ma'am. I've been on a stake-out all week."

"Why, that's perfectly all right," Carolina insisted as she attempted to shake a sticky tissue off her shoe. "Hidden Valley needs more brave officers of the law, such as yourself, to guard its lucky citizens."

Scruggs beamed under her praise. "Undercover. You know the drill."

"Undercover! Of course." Well that explained a lot. Perhaps this ambisexual look was some kind of costume.

"Suck-up," Hunt muttered into her ear, as he climbed out of the back seat after Carolina. Eyes rolling in disgust, he dragged her to the sidewalk by the wrist.

"At least I'm getting out of here tonight," she hissed, stumbling after him.

As the unlikely trio made their way toward the front door, two part-time cub reporters from the *Hidden Valley Gazette* leaped from the bushes and—bulbs flashing—pelted them with a barrage of questions.

"Officer Scruggs! Is it true that you have arrested Carolina Brubaker, Big Daddy Brubaker's niece, for trying to outrun the law?"

Carolina's mouth fell slack and she glanced at Hunt.

"Have you issued a breathalyzer test?"

"Officer Scruggs, how long did you have to chase them before finally capturing the suspects?"

"Now wait just a blasted minute." Eyes blazing, Carolina glared at the reporters. "I did not need a breathal—"

"Are you denying this drunken rampage?"

"What?"

Scooter's instamatic temporarily blinded Carolina. Blinking, she reached for Hunt to keep from losing her balance.

"Is it true that Brandon McGraw broke off your engagement, essentially setting off your drunken rampage?"

"I—*what?"*

Scooter got another shot, from a different angle.

"Ms. Brubaker, is this your first drunken rampage?"

"No!"

"So, it's *not* your first?"

"No!"

His arm circling her waist, Hunt propelled the flustered Carolina toward the door. "No comment. Listen, Scooter, you and Jasper go on home now. You can do your journalism homework some other time."

For just a split second, there, Hunt thought he saw a glimmer of gratitude in Carolina's eyes, but it was gone in the rabid twinkling with which it came.

At the police desk, they had to turn in their personal effects. Hunt couldn't help but notice that Scruggs took special care to apologize to Carolina for the inconvenience and to handle her belongings with TLC. His stuff, on the other hand, was jammed into an unmarked envelope and tossed into a junk drawer.

Next they moved on to have their fingerprints recorded.

Scruggs fawned over Carolina's snappy manicure, and offered her a premoistened towelette to clean her fingertips. She treated the weasel as if he'd just handed her the Hope diamond.

Hunt's lip lifted with derision. The woman had singlehandedly destroyed half of greater Hidden Valley, and now? Now she was mothering up to the town geek as if she hadn't a care in the world. Her behavior simply further cemented his attitude about women born to privilege. She had no conscience whatsoever. None of 'em did.

Save Big Daddy's wife, Miss Clarise Brubaker, of course. Now there was a lady. Too bad none of her Southern hospitality and charm had rubbed off on her niece. Hunt followed a chattering Carolina as they were herded from the print area and over to have their pictures taken for the record.

Scruggs posed Carolina just so, and even retook one that she insisted made her look bad. Hunt rubbed his temples. As if holding a card with a number on it and standing in front of a measurement chart could make one look good. From the picture area, they were escorted to the phone and allowed to make one call each. Neither Carolina nor Hunt were able to do more than leave a voice-mail message, as Big Daddy and Uncle Mike each had their own Independence Day duties to attend.

So, with Officer Scruggs's solemn promise that he'd let them know the minute their respective uncles called, he took them in through several very heavy, guarded doors to the jailhouse's only two cells. One small hall opened into two identical cells that Officer Scruggs called the Gray Bar Hotel. In reality, it was only a large, barred room divided down the center by yet another wall of bars.

After making sure they were familiar with their accommodations, Officer Scruggs locked them in and left. The resounding thud of the heavy hall door echoed for a good five seconds after he was gone.

Carolina slowly sagged down to her lumpy, blue-and-white-tick mattress and rubbed her wrist where the cuff had been. It was stuffy in here. Humid. Clearly they didn't waste air-conditioning on jailbirds. For a moment she watched as Hunt paced his space then, averting her eyes, gave the place a wary glance to get her bearings.

Each cell was about twelve by ten feet in size and, aside from the rock piles on metal frames that supposedly passed for beds, they each got a toilet, a sink and a chair. Although, she thought with a mirthless laugh, the very idea that she'd stoop to using that rust-ringed toilet even *with* complete privacy was ludicrous. She sighed and, turning on the water in her tiny sink, rinsed off her hands. Since there was no mirror, she could only guess at her disheveled appearance.

Cinder blocks made up the exterior walls, and concrete mortar oozed from between the joints. A row of fluorescent light fixtures lit the hall in front of the cells and, except for a lone bulb that hung in a caged fixture over her bed, that was it. Stark. Bare. Lonely.

Carolina shivered even in the heat. This was a horrible, terrible place. A horrible, terrible place, complete with a horrible, terrible neighbor. She stole a quick look at Hunt's brooding expression and shivered all over again.

She should have known that riding in his carriage would be a bad omen. From the minute he'd handed her into the back seat with Brandon, she'd felt his displeasure at her very existence. Then, when she and Brandon and begun discussing their private business and things had become a little...exuberant, she could sense his disapproval as strongly as if he'd turned around just like her daddy used to do and threatened to pull over to the side of the road and whup some butt.

Hello? She was a paying customer, for crying out loud.

And another thing…wasn't a driver supposed to go wherever the patron wanted? Okay, maybe she'd been a tad overzealous about following Brandon, but for heaven's sake, she'd been in shock. And hurt. Destroyed, actually. A new deluge of feelings threatened to overwhelm her. She pulled her upper lip between her teeth and bit back the tears. A smothering lump filled her throat, and she was sure it was a shard of her broken heart. How would she ever be able to face anyone again? Heretofore, she'd always thought the words 'died of a broken heart' or 'died of embarrassment' to be simply colorful old sayings. But here she was. Doing both.

Swinging her legs around to the other side of the bed, she turned her back on Hunt and swiped at the errant tear that trailed down her cheek. Just as soon as Big Daddy got her message, she'd be out of here, never to return.

Hunter Crenshaw, on the other hand, could stay here and rot.

Big Daddy Brubaker was chauffeured up to the police station's front entrance in a black stretch limousine. He'd been hosting a Fourth of July party up at the ranch when the call had come that his niece, Carolina, was being held in the local poky. At first, the shock had him and Miss Clarise frantic with worry, but when Judge Eustace Scruggs II, father of Officer Eustace Scruggs III, and an old friend of the family, had called with the facts, Big Daddy relaxed and took a little time to think things through.

When he was done studying the problem, he took a little more time to check on his guests. Made a toast to his country, chopped up the proverbial rug with his flushed and giggling wife, set off a few fireworks and then, when he was sure his niece had had sufficient time to ruminate upon her troubles, he'd headed to the police station.

"Jest let me out up 'air in front, Basil. I'll flag atcha when I'm ready to head home."

Though he'd never see five and a half feet without a boost, Big Daddy Brubaker had an imposing presence that garnered the complete respect of his sons, all eight of whom were well over six feet tall. As a young man, he'd been a real catch, handsome, dimpled, his body honed and solid with the hard work it takes to become a self-made billionaire in the oil business. He was tough, no doubt about it. But at the same time he had a gentle quality that made folks know that he was an honest man. Caring. Loving.

A family man.

Red cowboy boots carried him across the wooden boardwalk that led to a municipal complex, which—due to budget restraints—housed the city hall, the local police station, a small jail and the courthouse. The old-fashioned building was a square-roofed affair, complete with a corbelled Western facade straight out of an episode of *Gunsmoke*. Huge flower baskets hung between the porch posts, scenting the night air as Big Daddy moved past the old iron hitching posts from a bygone era, up the stairs and through the big glass double doors.

Inside, behind the lobby desk, all of the various municipal departments were housed in one large knotty-pine-paneled room and separated by a maze of gray tweed room dividers. The battleship-gray concrete floors enabled the night clerk, Selma Featherstone, to slide from window to window in her rolling chair, depending upon the needs of the patron.

At this hour, Selma sat behind the police station desk, reading a copy of the *World Globe,* and marveling over a baby who was born able to talk and sing. She patted her own very pregnant belly and wondered if there wasn't something to this "womb learning" stuff. As the bell over the door jangled, she dropped the paper and smiled.

"Hello, Big Daddy. How may I help you this holiday evenin'?"

"Selma darlin', I'm looking for the honorable Judge Scruggs. He phoned me 'bout an hour ago, and we decided to take a quick meetin'.

"Yes, sir. If you will just come with me to the courthouse, I'll call and see if he's in yet." Pushing off the counter, Selma rolled down three windows, picked a phone, punched up a complex series of numbers. The phone could be heard ringing in behind a partition directly over Selma's shoulder.

"Hello?" The judge's voice, though soft, filtered into the room. Even so, Selma focused on the phone in a most professional manner.

"Yes, sir, Your Honor. There is a Mr. Big Daddy Brubaker here to see you."

"Good. Please, show him back to my chambers."

"Yes, sir." Selma hung up, and signaled Big Daddy to join her behind the lobby desk. "The judge will see you now." She pointed to the partition behind her.

Judge Eustace Scruggs II was a mild-mannered pear of a man who was seated at his desk, peering through bottle-bottom glasses at the child's game on his computer. Befuddled, he jabbed and stabbed at the computer's keys.

Big Daddy entered the closet-size space with a cheerful, "Heya, Judge Scruggs."

"Well, hey there, Mr. Brubaker." The judge rotated around, pulled up a rolling stool and motioned for Big

Daddy to take a load off. He smacked the computer's screen with his knuckles. "My granddaughter left this disc in my drive, and I'll be darned if I can figure out how to get rid of it."

"Ya gotta go through the hedge of thorns before you can exit." Big Daddy pointed at the screen. "See there? It's a maze."

"Mmph." The judge squinted. "Well I'll be hang-doodled."

"Got a few granddaughters myself."

The judge dragged a fragile hand over his turkey-gobbler jowl and smiled. "So, Mr. Brubaker. Haven't seen you for longer than a wet week."

"I know it. But now I got this problem." Big Daddy frowned, his rubbery face wrinkling. He pulled a booted foot up over his knee and settled in for a powwow. "This summer, three of my brother's daughters are stay-ing with me for a little visit. Virginia, Carolina and Georgia. They all graduated from college within this last couple of years, so we invited 'em to come for some R&R before they jumped into the work force with both high heels this fall. But it seems that one of 'em got a little out of hand tonight."

"Right."

"Yeah. So, as you know, my niece, Carolina, is one of the two you've got holed up in that jail cell of yours." Big Daddy gave his throat a noisy clearing and leaned forward in his chair.

"You want me to set bail?"

"Well now, there's the rub. If her daddy ever found out that she broke the law, he'd just up and die of a bro-ken heart. But not till he took out some of his indigna-tion on the rest of us for not keeping her under closer supervision. See, he's about the most patriotic, law-abiding guy you'd ever want to meet. Even named his kids after the states of the Union. You can see an arrest wouldn't sit well."

"Mmm." Though the judge's voice was softer than Mr. Roger's grandma's, it carried a certain strength. And humor. "So it's best if he doesn't find out?"

Big Daddy nodded. "Right. Not just yet, anyway. I have dealt with my brother and his adventuresome off-spring a time or two before and I might—" the diminutive man looked like the cat that just dipped the canary in a light béarnaise sauce "—have a little plan."

"Well now," the judge said, arching a brow, "you know I'm always up for a little plannin'."

Claustrophobia had always been a bit of a bugaboo for Carolina, and having this annoying man in the next cell lazily hawking her every move was about to drive her out of her tree. He lay on his bed, hands folded under his head, his legs crossed at the ankles, as if he hadn't a care in the world other than chewing that infernal gum.

Carolina jumped to her feet and thrust out her hand. "Give me that gum."

"Why?"

"Because all that popping is annoying as hell."

"Well in that case, no. For a second there, I thought maybe you'd devised some clever plan involving gum to bust us outta this joint. But instead I see that you are simply concerned with the comfort of your precious ears." He folded his gum between his molars and let off another artillery-style round of pops.

"Stop it! I mean it! I've had enough."

Hunt reached into his pocket and pulled out another stick and stuffed it into his mouth. "Gum?" he offered and held the remaining pack out to her. "I find it soothing."

"Ooo." Carolina stood and marched to the door of her cell and peered down the hall, and then checked her watch as she had done a number of times that evening. "Where is my uncle?"

"Maybe he's baking you a cake with a file in it. From scratch. Those things take time."

She tilted her head and squinted at him through haughty eyes. As if she had the time or inclination to do her nails now. And fear had completely killed her appetite. She'd never understood that old "file in the cake" thing anyway, so she ignored his reference. "Yeah, well I don't see your precious uncle Mike rushing over here to bail you out."

They fell silent. But only for a moment. Hunt popped his gum. The larger wad was noisier than ever.

Carolina rushed to her cell door and gave it a fierce rattle. *"Hello,"* she shouted. "Officer *Scruggs!* I'm ready to go *home* now." When there was no answer, she took off her boot and beat a vicious tattoo on the bars of her cell with its heel. "Hey! *Help! Please,* I need to get *out* of here! I watch *Law and Order!* I know I get at least *one* phone call. Voice mail doesn't really count, right? *Hello? It's time for my phone call!"*

Except for the occasional crack of Hunt's gum, silence echoed.

Hunt pulled his Stetson down over his eyes and nose. "Scruggs can't hear you."

"How do you know?"

"I know a lot of stuff."

"Yeah? Well you can just stuff your stuff. You don't know anything."

"I know that you are a selfish brat and that's why your boyfriend dumped you."

Carolina gasped. "You know no such thing!"

Hunt lifted the brim of his hat and eyed her, his expression speaking volumes. "I also know they can't hear you because the walls are two feet thick. I helped build the dumb place. I oughta know."

Carolina paused, and after some thought, decided to use this opportunity to ferret out information on Scruggs. "You and Officer Scruggs built this place?"

"Nope. Scruggs was in the Police Academy back when Billy Jack Construction built this place. I work for them when they're short."

Scruggs. Not he. Not she. Always simply "Scruggs." Funny. Not once had she heard a single person offer a clue as to his—or her—gender. It was the weirdest thing.

She surreptitiously glanced at Hunt through the curtain of her hair. Old blowhard over there claimed to know everything. Certainly he'd know the answer. But she'd be darned if she'd come right out and ask. He'd humiliate her to no end over that. Maybe she could finesse him in to giving the information away through conversation.

"So—" she gave her head a casual toss "—how long have you known Officer Scruggs?"

"Went to grade school together."

"Oh. Did you play sports on the same team?

"With Stacy?"

"Who?"

"That's what we called Scruggs in grade school."

Stacy. *Hmm.* The actor, Stacy Keech came to mind. Didn't he sometimes play a lawman? On the other hand, she had a sorority sister named Stacy.

"And sports?" Hunt guffawed. "That's a laugh. Nah, Scruggs was a cops and robbers kind of kid. Always shooting some kind of rubber band gun at the 'bad kids.'"

"At *you,* you mean."

Grinning, Hunt popped his gum.

As she wrapped a long strand of hair around her index finger, Carolina wondered how she was ever going to get on Officer Scruggs's good side at this rate. Could she play the sister card? Or should she simply flirt her way out of here? The only thing she knew for certain was that Scruggs held the key to her freedom until Big Daddy arrived.

"Judge Scruggs." Big Daddy—using a special gold tool, engraved with his initials—nipped the tips off two premium cigars. "I don't ordinarily play favorites among my kids, but out of all my nieces and nephews, I'm ashamed to admit that I'm a tad partial to Carolina. She's fun loving and sweet as the day is long and would never trouble anyone on purpose. However, she's one high-spirited little filly with a helluva temper." Big Daddy handed the judge his cigar and pulled out a lighter. "She raised hell and built the basement, ya know what I mean?"

There was a far-off, muffled racket coming from the direction of the jail. *"Hellooo? I'm ready to go hooome nowww."*

The judge puffed on the pricey import with satisfaction. "Yup," he blew a series of impressive rings at the ceiling, "if that's her bellerin' back 'air in her cell, she's got a set-a lungs on her."

Big Daddy nodded, his cigar bobbing in the flame. "Mm. That she do, indeedy. She's not bad exactly, just impulsive. But at the same time I'm afraid she worries her daddy over things such as this."

"Lordy, I hear ya. My youngest daughter is a real hell-raiser, too."

If Big Daddy wondered which one of the kids—in the framed photo of the most interesting, bespectacled pack of pear-shaped, moon-faced youngsters he'd ever laid eyes on—was the judge's youngest daughter, he made no comment.

"And Hunt, no—" Big Daddy settled his hat back on his head and waved his cigar "—he's your other prisoner. He works for me. And he's a different kind of a deal altogether. He's a real type-A workaholic. Why I'm afraid he's gonna work himself half to death someday, without stopping to smell a single dadburn rose. When he's not working my place, he's busy givin' somebody else a hand. That's what he was doing tonight, according to his uncle Mike."

"Mmm. Kinda like my boy, Eustace."

"Uh. Yeah. Right. So, along with the other plans we've discussed, it's my opinion that perhaps a night in the hoosegow might just mellow both of 'em out a hair."

Judge Scruggs took a placid puff from his stogie. "Check. So let's review, just to make sure we're on the same page. I can have 'em for a month's community service?"

"Yep. I'll arrange for Hunt to take some much-needed vacation time, and I'll make sure Carolina's daddy don't get any messages for him to send along a lawyer to get her off the hook."

"Okay. We'll set the hearing for Monday week, and I'll sentence them right then."

"She's gonna squawk," Big Daddy warned and gave his cigar a pensive gnawing.

"Won't be the first."

"She'll need supervision."

"I'll put Junior on the beat."

"Good, good. Okay, Judge, I guess that oughta do it. Thanks for goin' along with me on this." Big Daddy stood and backed away from his chair.

"I'll just see you out of my office and to the lobby."

"Why don't ya see me out to my place? I got a little

Fourth of July celebration goin' on, couple of beef on the spit and the usual fireworks until sunup. We can swing by and pick up your missus on the way out."

"Now that sounds like a fine time." The judge followed Big Daddy. "But first just let me have Junior tell the prisoners that they'll be spending the night."

Chapter Three

The unmistakable sound of someone unlocking the series of doors that led to the jail had Carolina springing off her bed and rushing to her cell door. Was it Officer Scruggs? She hoped so, although not knowing the answer to the gender bender was making her a little crazy. Nervously she nibbled at her lip and figured she had a fifty-fifty chance whichever way she went, so she'd decided—after thoroughly weighing the evidence—to go with female. A small backwater like Hidden Valley would probably need tough cops to handle the rowdys that cut loose on Friday and Saturday nights. As a man, Scruggs seemed a little weak. But as a woman? Oh, yeah. She'd make one kick-butt chick.

Keys jangled just outside the door to the jail and then scraped about in the lock.

"Someone's coming."

Hunt lolled his head and arched an indolent brow. "Who?"

"How should I know? Maybe it's—" she narrowed her eyes and studied Hunt's face "—Stacy?"

"Stacy?"

"*Stacy?* Our arresting officer's first name, according to you."

"Oh. Yeah. Stacy. Right." Hunt dragged a hand through his hair, settled his Stetson just so and sat up.

"Maybe she's coming to let us go."

A small frown pulled duel hash marks between Hunt's eyes as he stared at her. Then a slow smile traversed his mouth. He swung his feet to the floor and stretched as if he'd spent a lazy evening relaxing at home. "Yeah. As usual, you're probably right."

Carolina stamped her feet and tugged her pant legs back down over her boots. Then, as she smoothed her hair and straightened her collar, she inhaled with smug satisfaction. "My uncle has probably posted my bail already."

Hunt let loose with another semiautomatic spray of gum shot and gave his jaw a thoughtful scratch. "Yeah, that's probably just what's happened, you always bein' right and all."

Chin jutting, she snapped her head toward the door and fixed her gaze there. His sarcasm would not dull her enthusiasm. After what seemed like an inordinate length of time, the keys ceased jangling and the heavy door swung open.

"Officer Scruggs!" Carolina pushed her face to the bars and peered down the narrow hall to where Scruggs's pear shape stood silhouetted in the doorway. "Am I ever glad to see you!"

Officer Scruggs's chest expanded.

"In fact—" she shook the bars "—I've never been so happy to see anybody in my *life!*"

A heady smile quirked the officer's normally tight lips.

Crooking her finger, she beckoned to the officer in a confidential manner. "You've just gotta get me outta here right away, ma'am."

Hunt hooted. *"Ma'am?"*

Scruggs's tiny smile collapsed.

"Oh!" Her gaze darted to Officer Scruggs and then, with murder, to Hunt. Like the mercury in a thermometer at midsummer, a molten heat rushed from her toes and settled in her cheeks. *"Gram! Mamm-Oh!-Gram!* I have an emergency *mammogram!"* she furiously backpedaled. "Right now! On the double, people! I need out! These babies—" she thrust her breasts through the bars "—are nothing to fool around with!"

She bared all of her teeth into a blinding smile and thought about how she'd like to wring, no choke, no twist…make that *tear* Hunt's head off his neck just as soon as she got the chance. He'd known she'd mistaken Scruggs for a woman, and yet he'd let her embarrass them both. The maggot.

She hated him with the fury of a thousand bonfires.

She'd make sure Big Daddy handed him his pink slip today.

With a step back, she spun to face Officer Scruggs and waved an airy hand in hopes of skimming over the identity crisis. Issuing a confidential wink she said, "I hate to discuss female troubles with one so manly as yourself—"

Behind her, she could sense Hunt's disgust.

"—but actually this was the only time they could fit me in. For my *mam*mogram. Really. I must be on my way. An ounce of prevention is worth a pound of cure, as they say…." she babbled.

Hunt's voice startled her. "On the evening of the Fourth of July?" Seemed he was suddenly standing at the wall of bars that divided their cells. "You expect us to believe that you have a mammogram scheduled tonight?"

"No!" She scowled over her shoulder. "For your information, I have it first thing on the morning of the fifth, and I need to…to…prepare myself."

His expression skeptical, Hunt's eyes slid to her chest. "Big job?"

"Shut up."

"Call the doctor, Scruggs. Find out if she's just trumping up some excuse to bust outta here. Forgive the pun." He slapped his knee and hooted.

"Oh, please. There is certainly no need to bother the doctor at this late hour." Carolina issued some tinkly laughter. "He needs his sleep. I want him to be…fresh. For…the, uh, procedure."

Hunt smirked. "You want your doctor *fresh?* During your breast exam?"

"Would you stick a sock in your piehole?"

"I will if you will."

As they argued, Officer Scruggs was once again all business. "I've come to let you know," he interrupted, "that your respective uncles are unavailable at the moment, so you'll both be spending the night here, at the Gray Bar."

"What?" Hunt planted his fists on his hips.

"S-s-spend the night? Here?" Carolina sputtered after Officer Scruggs's retreating back. "Together? With…*him?*"

"Yes, ma'am." Scruggs turned at the door and nodded at Carolina with contrition. "I'm sorry, but it's judge's orders." His gaze turned smug when it landed on Hunt.

Carolina gripped the bars and rattled her door. "But…but…I want to talk to the judge! Or at the very least call my uncle!"

"They are both unavailable this evening. Right now I've got a Code 7 downtown."

"But…but—"

The slam of the door echoed with finality.

Flopping back down on his bed, Hunt adjusted his hat over his face.

Carolina stared at him, dumbfounded. He was just going to *lie* there? "Aren't you going to do something?"

"Yeah. I'm gonna take a little nap."

"You can't take a nap!"

"Watch me."

What had started out as gentle, sonorous—nearly comforting in its regularity—breathing was now becoming a nasal concert with all the charm of a diesel engine. In the cell next door, Hunt was sleeping like a baby, and frankly, it irritated Carolina to no end. For what seemed like eons, she'd lain there, trying to doze off. But *no-oo-o*. Even in his sleep, Hunt had the last word. Ooo, how he frustrated her.

She jerked to her side and yanked the covers up over her head. At least the sheets seemed vermin free. Just before Hunt had nodded off, Selma Featherstone had given them fresh linens for their beds and blankets stamped with the words Property of Hidden Valley County Jail. The very chatty, not to mention very pregnant, woman had also microwaved up a couple of frozen meat loaf dinners and some instant coffee for them.

The caffeine didn't seem to faze Hunt.

Carolina dove under her pillow, but it still did nothing to muffle the noise of his slumber. She wondered suddenly if that rodent from Officer Scruggs's car could claw its way into her cell. And she wondered if it could get up onto her bed. Fear shot up her spine and she shivered. Would it bite? What if it had rabies?

In the dim glow of the remaining hall light, Carolina could see that Hunt was sleeping on his back, one arm thrown up over his face, the other dangling over the edge of the bed. How could he sleep like that? Wasn't he afraid of rodents nibbling on his fingertips?

Carolina tried counting sheep.

Loudly snoring sheep.

Nothing worked.

"Pssst. Hunt."

"Zzzzz."

"Hunt!"

"Zzzzz."

"For crying out loud! Hunt, stop snoring!"

"Zzzzz."

"Turn over! I'm not kidding. Stop it, or I'll, I'll…" Forgetting the rodent factor, she leaped out of bed, snagged one of her cowboy boots and stomped to the wall of bars that separated their cells. Taking aim, she fired the boot across the room and hit the wall just above his head. The boot smacked the cinderblocks with a satisfying *thwack,* then fell to Hunt's face.

"Whaaa?" He snatched up the boot and sat up, blinking and dazed. Seeing Carolina standing there, with her arms folded across her chest, he brandished the boot. "What the hell is this for?"

"I can't sleep."

He flung the boot at the floor. "That's not my problem."

"It's your problem when it is you who are keeping me awake."

With a groan, Hunt flopped back onto the mattress. "Go to *bed.* It's easier to sleep that way."

"I might, if you would stop your infernal snoring."

"I don't snore," he mumbled as he arranged his covers under his chin.

"Yes, you do."

"No. I don't." He squinted at her, challenging her to disagree.

"How do you know?

"I have it on good authority, okay?"

Was this cretin married? She'd never paused to consider that. At any rate, she pitied the woman foolish enough to hitch her star to his wagon.

"Okay. You don't snore. Kindly stop breathing at the top of your lungs." Carolina harrumphed and flounced back to bed where she sat wrapped in her blanket.

The silence was almost more disturbing than the snoring. At least when Hunt snored, she could be sure he was asleep.

"Pssst."

Hunt sighed. "What now?"

"Are you awake?

"Am I snoring?"

"No."

"Then leave me alone."

"Why didn't they let us out?"

"How should I know? Small town politics. Maybe Scruggs wants your body. All that mammogram stuff turned him on."

"Very funny. Why didn't you tell me he was a man?" Disgruntled, Carolina pulled her feet up underneath her legs.

"You didn't ask."

"So you just let me make a fool of myself."

"You do that just fine on your own."

"So you let me make a fool of Scruggs."

"He does that just fine by himself."

"You're really not a very nice person, are you?"

That cracked him up. "Oh, that's rich. You calling the kettle black."

"I'm a perfectly nice person."

"Oh, yeah. You just oozed sweetness and light back there in my poor carriage. No wonder what's-his-face ran away."

"You do not have a clue about Brandon's and my relationship."

"Puleeze. I know your so-called boyfriend is ready to take on the third woman in your family. Seems to me you're both better off without each other."

"I suppose you know all of this because *you've* been happily married for years."

"Nope.

"Aha. *Un*happily married for years. That figures."

"Nope."

"Divorced. I knew it."

"Nope."

"You killed your wife."

"No!" His eyes darted to the ceiling in disgust. He sighed, seeming to sense that she'd badger him until he clarified his marital status. "Just never tied the knot."

"Now why didn't I guess that first?"

"Just slow, I guess."

"Do you ever say anything nice to anyone?"

"Do you?"

The dim light of the single bulb in the hall filtered into their cells, giving Carolina only a shadowy peek at Hunt's face, and for a second it almost looked as if he was smiling. Impossible. He was too ornery.

"That was one humdinger of a party last night, Brubaker." Judge Scruggs held open the courthouse door for Big Daddy, and both men meandered into the judge's chambers. The judge rummaged up a couple of clean mugs for some much-needed caffeine.

Big Daddy leaned against the coffee cart while the

judge shrugged out of his windbreaker and tossed it over a chair. "Yeahup. I gotta say that one'll go down in the books. I think Harley Halverson is still there, though the cleanup crew is nearly done."

"Yeah. Old Harley. He's a competitive one, when it comes to riding the mechanical bull." The judge fiddled with the filters, struggled with the coffee can and sloshed water onto the floor. "How do you like your coffee?"

"This morning?" Mouth wide, Big Daddy's yawn was the sound of noisy contentment. "Strong enough to eat with a fork."

"Will do 'er. If I can figure out how to work this infernal machine."

"Gotta push the power button there, Judge."

"Oh."

"Too bad my niece had to miss all the fun. Wonder how she and Hunt fared last night?"

"Well, if that's her screeching like a plucked jaybird back there, I'd say not so well."

From off in the next room, the distant sounds of a cursing muleskinner's convention approached. Jangling keys scraping about in a series of locks brought these heated voices steadily closer.

And louder.

"…would have been ready ages ago if you hadn't insisted on sitting there, leering at me while I brushed my teeth."

"Though you are the center of my universe, I wasn't leering at your damned teeth."

"Yes you were! And it's positively unnerving."

"Honey, even if you had you been standing there stark naked and 'preparing yourself' for your *mam*mogram, I *still* wouldn't have been tempted to leer. That big mouth of yours kills any desire a guy would have to look twice at your precious mammos, let alone any-thing north of there."

"Excuse me? You are in such denial. I see the way you look at me when you think no one else sees. Heaven only knows what's going on in that nasty little head of yours."

Hunt guffawed. "If you want to know what I'm thinking this very second, I'll be only too happy to tell you that last night had to go down in history as the *worst* night I have ever spent under the same roof with a female of *any* species! And, as a matter of fact, I'm not the only one who snores, honey—"

Carolina gasped. "That's a damned lie!"

"Oh, really?" Hunt threw back his head, let his mouth fall open and gargled up a few rusty snorts.

The last door to the jail burst open and, as they ex-ploded forth, Officer Scruggs corralled them the best he could into the holding area to complete the paperwork for their release on bail. Behind the gray partition that separated the judge's chamber from the rest of the build-ing, Big Daddy and Judge Scruggs exchanged glances.

"Looks like they could both use a little mellowing out," the judge said.

"Mmm-hmm. A month together, learnin' to get along and be good citizens and such. Be good for 'em. Yessir."

"Probably could use a course in anger management. I could throw that into the deal," Judge Scruggs of-fered.

Big Daddy shrugged. "Sign 'em up."

Together their heads cocked toward the ruckus.

"...as if your nasal explosions are some kind of pic-nic!"

"Oh, yeah? Well, you also talk in your sleep, doll-face." Hunt affected a high, whiney voice. "Brandon! Get your butt back here, Brandon! *Brrraaannndon!*"

Carolina blew a raspberry at Hunt.

Judge Scruggs handed Big Daddy a cup of coffee. "Junior's about ready to turn them over to your care. You'll have them back Monday week, for their hearing?"

Big Daddy's eyes forked with undisguised glee. "Wouldn't miss it."

Carolina stood at one of the many windows in her elegant suite at the Circle BO. She stared, unseeing, at the lush gardens beyond the mansion's rolling lawn. Though she was surrounded by ultimate luxury, she was utterly miserable. Funny how wealth did nothing to soothe a broken heart. At the knock on the door to her suite, Carolina moved across the room, pulled on the knob and gestured her younger sister inside.

"Hi." Georgia looked a little perplexed as she walked into the room. "You sounded so urgent I didn't even finish my breakfast. And it was good, too. Cook makes bacon just the way I like—" She frowned. "Why are you still wearing the same clothes you wore last night?"

"I just got home." Carolina dropped to her bed and motioned for Georgia to join her.

"You're *just* getting home?" There was an underlying note of censure in Georgia's voice as she settled onto the end of the mattress and turned to study her disheveled sister.

"Yes. I had to stop on the way for a quick mammogram. Long story."

"You did. *This* morning. A…mammogram?"

"Yes. And don't go acting all suspicious and holier than thou." Her eyes narrowed. "You know perfectly well I wasn't with Brandon."

"I…do?"

"Don't you?"

"Do I?"

"You tell me."

Georgia's nose wrinkled with her confusion. "Tell you what?"

Carolina sighed and flopped back against the huge pile of pillows at her headboard. "Don't you read the paper? Certainly the whole sordid story must be splashed all over the headlines."

"Carolina, you're not making a bit of sense." Leaning forward, elbows to knees, Georgia propped her chin in her hands. "Why don't you start from the beginning and tell me what happened."

"You mean you really don't know?"

"Know *what?*"

Carolina sighed and regarded her sister's impatient expression. Was this the face of sinister betrayal? Or the face of simple bewilderment? She and Georgia had always been so close. She'd hate for anything like the affections of a man to come between them.

Georgia reached out and gently took her sister's hand. "Whatever it is, it can't be that horrible."

Carolina lifted a lone eyelid and peered at her sister. "Oh, sure. Not for *you.*"

"Carolina—" Georgia was growing weary of this verbal volleyball "—just spit it out."

"Okay." Carolina inhaled dramatically. "I know about you and Brandon."

Georgia blinked. "Me and Brandon who?"

"McGraw. Your soon-to-be boyfriend."

"My soon-to-be *what?*"

"Sorry to ruin the surprise, but he's going to ask you out soon."

"He wants to date *me?*"

"Uh-huh. Says he's in love with you."

"In…" Georgia fell back on the bed and laughed at the ceiling, "*love* with me? Okay. I get it. You're kidding. Har-de-har. Very funny. Is this your way of telling me that he popped the question last night, or what? Because frankly, I'm a little confused."

"You're confused? *You're* confused?"

"Uh…yeah?" Georgia raised up to an elbow. "Brandon? McGraw? In love with *me?* But how could that *be?* I've only spoken to him a handful of times, and even then, I was in a hurry and rather curt."

"Super. He seems to respect rude people."

"Okay. Would you please start this whole stupid story from the beginning?"

Her sigh heavy, Carolina began her tragic tale with the purchase of her new boots yesterday afternoon.

"And so now I have to go back to court this coming Monday and find out what kind of fines I have, or whatever. Hopefully, the judge will have mercy on me and let me off with a warning, because let me tell you, between getting arrested, and ending up on the front page of the paper, I've had enough punishment to last a lifetime."

Carolina dunked her teabag in the steaming water as she looked across the tiny kitchen's table at her newly married older sister, Ginny. "And the worst part of it is that, that Hunt yahoo who works here—"

"Hunter Crenshaw." Ginny's arched brow carried a gentle reprimand. "My husband's best friend? The cowboy in the bunkhouse next door?"

Looking as if she'd just bitten into an unripe lemon, Carolina said, "Yeah, him. Anyway, I had to spend the night in jail with him. You simply cannot believe the stuff that comes out of that man's mouth! He's so arrogant, and condescending a complete horse's *boob*—"

"Oh, really, Carolina." Ginny's smile was serene. "Hunt is a wonderful man with one of the most solid work ethics I've ever encountered. If you'd give him half a chance I think you'd find—"

"What? That he was Rosemary's baby?" Carolina snorted. "Has marriage made you so soft in the head?"

Though Ginny had eloped with Colt Bartlett, one of Big Daddy's ranch hands, last month and now lived in a tiny bunkhouse at the edge of a pond in the middle of a dusty cattle ranch, she'd never looked happier. Marriage certainly seemed to agree with her sister, as, for once, Carolina actually felt as if she were talking to Ginny sister to sister, instead of sister to psychologist.

The transformation was nothing short of a miracle. When she and her sisters had arrived at the beginning of summer for some much-needed R&R, Ginny had been more of a basket case than the patients she coached in her stress seminars. Carolina envied her sister's marital bliss and the tranquil expression she now wore.

"Not soft in the head. Soft in the heart." Ginny picked up a cookie and broke it in two. "Actually, I think marriage has made me see people a little more clearly. I think I'm a pretty good judge of character these days. Listen, honey, Hunt is Colt's oldest friend, and honestly he's very charming. In fact, he's going to be here any second now, for lunch. Why don't you stay and get to know him?"

"Yeech. Have you been smoking this stuff?" Carolina flipped a teabag at her sister. "If Hunt is on the way, I'm outta here."

"Too late." Ginny smiled. "They're here."

The sound of boots thudding up the back steps had the tiny hairs on Carolina's arms suddenly standing on end. She glanced out the sliding-glass door. Oh, crud. It was her new brother-in-law.

And his loathsome best friend.

Chapter Four

As he followed his buddy, Colt Bartlett, across the back deck to the kitchen, Hunt felt the tiny hairs on the nape of his neck stand at attention. There was something peculiar in the air…he couldn't put his finger on it, but he suddenly found himself battling a flaming bout of acid indigestion. Strange. He'd felt perfectly fine until he'd mounted the steps to Colt and Ginny's bunkhouse, and then *whammo*. Antagonism.

Irritation.

He caught a glimpse through the sliding-glass door of the unmistakable profile reflected in a mirror.

Carolina.

His stomach clenched. What was *she* doing here? He grabbed Colt's arm and yanked his friend back away from the door and around the side of the cabin.

"Is this some kind of joke?" Hunt could feel the veins on his neck straining at his collar. He hadn't planned on seeing that woman until a week from today, and even that was a lifetime too soon.

Colt's stare was blank. "What? What's wrong?"

"*She's* here, that's what's wrong."

"But—"

"Just tell me you're not going to force me to have lunch with that viper."

"Now, just a doggone minute." Agitated, Colt lowered his voice and held a finger under his friend's nose. "That 'viper' just happens to be my wife and if you have some kind of a problem with her I'll thank you not to—"

"Not Ginny. Her sister. Carolina." Hunt jerked a thumb over his shoulder. "The kook."

Colt's expression relaxed into a grin. "Carolina's here?"

"Oh, like you didn't know." Hunt's eyes narrowed. "You're not trying to fix me up with her or something, are you?"

Colt hooted. "Sheya. Right. Get over yourself. Come on, Ginny made beef stew and corn bread for lunch. She'll be really honked off if you don't stay and eat." He paused and took a step toward Hunt. "Look, I really don't know why Carolina's here, but I doubt it's to see you. You're a big boy. Buck up. A few minutes in the same room won't kill you."

Hunt merely grunted.

Without waiting for a more articulate reply, Colt strode to the door, threw it open, headed straight for his wife and placed his lips on her neck.

Vacillating, Hunt stood at the entrance inhaling the heavenly aroma. On the one hand, his belly was growling and Ginny made corn bread with sweet cream butter that was out of this world. On the other hand, just being in the same building with her spoiled brat of a sister was enough to kill even the heartiest appetite. If he left now, he could run over to his place and rummage up a jar of pickles and a few Nilla wafers.

His baser instincts won out and against his better judgment, Hunt stepped inside. "Ginny," he said with a nod.

"Hi, Hunt." There was a warm smile in her voice as Ginny stood and moved to the oven.

How, Hunt wondered, *could two sisters be so vastly different?*

"Have a seat, hon. You remember my younger sister? Carolina?"

"I never forget a snore."

"I do not snore!" Carolina snapped her napkin across her lap.

"Good, good," Ginny murmured. Mouthwatering steam belched forth from the oven. "I've invited her to stay and have lunch with us. Colt, sweetheart, will you be a love and get the salad out of the refrigerator?"

Colt gave his wife's derriere a very fancy, somewhat lingering patting on his way to the fridge. "You betcha, babe.

"Hun-*ney,* not in front of the guests."

"What guests? I don't see any guests. I do see a couple of jailbirds."

"Shh!" Ginny had to look away to keep from laughing.

Salad in hand, Colt paused on his way back to the table and emitted a lusty growl into his bride's ear. The delighted squeals and randy snorts had Hunt and Carolina looking alternately at the floor and ceiling.

"Co-o-lt, stop it. You're going to make me drop the corn bread."

"Sorry, babe. It's just that you smell so doggoned delicious!"

Hunt squirmed in his seat. For some reason the newlywed banter that he normally didn't really notice, now irritated him today. Especially with the frigid Carolina sitting right across the table. He stole a glance in her direction.

As usual, she looked as if she'd just emerged from the ice-maiden beauty salon. Not a blamed hair out of place and her clothes alone no doubt cost more than his monthly car payment. Too bad she was such an uppity snob because she wasn't that bad looking, really.

Big old eyes as blue as forget-me-nots in the spring, and a perfect, narrow nose. Her full lips curled over orthodontically correct teeth and her cheeks were high and applelike above a jaw in the shape of a softly rounded heart. The only part of her anatomy that *was* softhearted, he was sure.

Anyhow, there was nothing really all that unusual about her face. However, even though there were no scars, no wrinkles and no freckles to give her distinction, she was exceedingly memorable. She only wore a smidgen of lipstick and some professional gold streaks in her long, blond hair because she was pretty much a classic beauty.

And she knew it.

Hunt couldn't ever imagine *her* pulling a steamy pan of corn bread out of the oven. Might wreck a nail. And he certainly couldn't imagine nuzzling that long patrician neck. The ice chip on her shoulder would no doubt freeze his tongue to her flesh like a kid at the flagpole in winter.

So then. Why were his thoughts headed in *that* direction? He could barely stand to look at her, and here he was, noticing her flawless complexion and wondering if her lips were really as soft as they looked.

Insane.

She drove him posilutely out-of-his-gourd insane.

"Beat any horses lately?" he asked, in an effort to turn the direction of his lascivious thoughts.

"Colt?" Carolina ignored Hunt's barb and helped herself to a serving of Caesar salad. "Certainly, with all the nice men who work for Big Daddy on this ranch, you could find yourself a new friend."

"Bread?" Ginny chirped at Hunt.

"Thank you." Hunt took the basket, helped himself and then held it out to Carolina. "Bread?"

"Yes, please."

Without ceremony, Hunt lobbed a hunk into the middle of her salad.

"Gee, thanks."

"Oh, now don't go keeping a civil tongue in your head, just for me."

"Okay. And don't keep from taking a flying leap into the pond on my account."

"So, Ginny—" Hunt's tone was conversational as he helped himself to a bubbly hot bowl of beef stew "—you're a psychologist, right? How come you haven't cured your sister yet?"

Carolina broke open a packet of sweetener and added it to her iced tea. "She can't practice on family. But I'm sure your peculiarities would make for a dandy case study, wouldn't they, sis?"

"Sweetheart—" Ginny inclined her head at her husband "—could you pass the stew? You all might want to try the stew before salting it. I was a little heavy-handed with the spice."

"Mmm." Colt winked. "That's the way I like you best."

Smile soft, Ginny said, "You are so sweet. Now. Let's all join hands for grace."

Automatically Hunt reached for Carolina's hand and, for some bizarre reason, the minute his work-roughened hand enveloped hers, a flash of gooseflesh raced down her arm and danced across her right thigh. *Weird.* Probably just their animosity taking on a life of its own, she reasoned. Carolina ducked her head and tried to concentrate as Colt thanked the good Lord above for the food and the hands that prepared it and for the fine fellowship they were sharing that day.

After Hunt and Colt had wolfed down a hearty lunch and left, Ginny and Carolina lingered at the table over cups of coffee.

"I simply don't understand what it is about Hunt that gets you in such a snit," Ginny murmured after a sip of coffee.

Carolina slid down in her seat and beat a tattoo on the table with her spoon. "Okay. I've been giving that a lot of thought and I think I have the answer."

"And?"

"I hate him."

"Okay, then." Ginny smiled. "On a different but somewhat similar note, what exactly happened between you and Brandon? I thought you two had something special going on there."

"So did I." Carolina sighed. "But he claims that Georgia is more his cup of tea, and if that's the case, there's not much I can do."

"I guess not. Still…" Deep in thought, Ginny propped her elbows on the table and held her mug between her fingertips. "You say Brandon wants to date Georgia? That's unusual."

"Why? You think he still carries a torch for you?"

"No!" Ginny laughed.

"Then you think he's really in love with Georgia?"

With a vigorous shake of her head, Ginny set down her mug. "I really don't think so. But, in my research,

I have heard of men who date every woman in a given family because the grass is always greener, so to speak."

Carolina groaned. "I'm a dead lawn with a police record. Can't you say something to cheer me up? Anything."

"I might be able to help you out, but you have to promise not to tell a soul. Nobody. At all. Got that?"

Carolina took a slug of coffee and shrugged. "Sure. What the hey. I can keep a secret."

"Promise?"

"Okay, already. I promise."

"I think I might be expecting a baby."

"What?"

"What?" Georgia's giddy scream reverberated around Carolina's bedroom, where they were once again lounging on her bed, later that same evening. "Ginny's having a *baby!*" Thrashing with joy, Georgia nearly bounced her sister to the floor.

"Shh! You can't tell anybody. If she finds out I told you, then she'll kill me. Plus she hasn't been to the doctor yet, but the home pregnancy tests are usually pretty accurate. Even so, don't say a word. She wants to wait till she sees the doctor before she tells anyone."

Carolina smiled to herself. Ginny had to know she'd tell Georgia. Everyone knew that Carolina always told Georgia everything.

And now that she and Georgia had had their heart-to-heart, she knew Georgia still told her everything, too. Even though, in regard to Brandon, there hadn't been much to tell. The very idea that Brandon had claimed he was in love with Georgia of all people—especially in light of the fact that they barely knew each other—still had them both confounded. After a lengthy hash session, both women had come to the conclusion that Brandon was simply grasping at any weapon to fling at Carolina during their fight, and Georgia's name had simply popped out.

Still, the fact that Brandon may have switched his allegiance—even in the heat of the moment—stung, but Carolina could hardly blame her sister for his fickle sense of timing.

"A baby." Georgia sighed. "That's just so…thrilling! Oh, I think I'm gonna cry."

"Yeah. I know. I'm really happy for her, too." Carolina's smile was wistful.

"Oh, honey. But you're sad for yourself." Georgia gave her head a sympathetic bob. "So, you went over to Ginny's this afternoon to figure out the Brandon thing?"

"Mmm-hmm."

"And did you come to any conclusions?"

"She says that Brandon is some kind of pathological dater, or something, and he won't be happy till he dates everyone in our family."

"Yeesh. I don't think Mom is going to like that." Georgia snorted and that got them giggling.

"Neither is Dad."

"Wow, just think! Brandon could end up being our stepfather!"

"Mom would probably spit on a napkin and try to clean his face after dinner."

They both fell back on the bed and rolled around in fits of laughter. When the hilarity and jokes at Brandon's expense had died, Carolina propped herself up on a pillow and regarded her sister. "So, what will you do if Brandon comes over here tonight and starts the wooing process?"

"What do you suggest?"

"Well, you could send him packing. Or—"

"Or what?"

"I don't know. I guess you could see where it goes. Brandon's really not such a bad guy. And maybe you two are meant for each other."

"Really? I hardly think so."

"Phew. Good. Just testing. That would be hideous, huh?"

"Mmm-hmm."

"Yep." Carolina stared at the ceiling for a moment, then blurted, "Hunt was at Ginny's for lunch today."

"Hunt the horrible?"

"Yep." Carolina had no idea why she'd mentioned him to Georgia. Other than the fact that she told Georgia everything.

"And, how is Hunt?"

"Horrible."

"Ah. So lunch must have been super-enjoyable."

"I don't know what it is about him." Carolina tossed her hands up, then let them thud on the bed. "I've always just detested him. Ever since he started working here in the summers, back when we were in high school. He's so…holier than thou. The way he looks at me, you'd think I was some kind of kitten killer or something."

"And it's always been like this between you two?"

"Totally chilly. In fact, I don't think he's ever even said 'boo' to me, before last Friday night."

"But you've spoken to him in the past?"

"Heck no. Why would I give him the time of day?"

"So—" the furrow between Georgia's brow deepened "—you're mad because he's never spoken to you, but you've never spoken to him."

"Well, yeah."

Georgia smacked her sister on the arm.

"What?" Carolina cried. "It's the principle!"

They both fell into another fit of laughter and then decided to call Ginny and talk about the baby.

"But I *want* to pay for the damage," Hunt told his uncle Mike as they labored together over the waxing and polishing of Mike's fleet of carriages the following evening.

"Don't worry about it, son. That's what insurance is for."

"No. Insurance is for an accident. This was more like a blond tantrum. With dents."

Uncle Mike chuckled. "C'mon, now, son. Old Blue's back. The carriage is only a bit bunged up. No harm done on my end. Stop fretting."

The twilight sun slanted through the windows of the carriage house that sat just two blocks off Main Street in Hidden Valley's quaint historic district. The stuffy old building smelled of motor oil and musty timber and the pungent carriage cleaning supplies.

Hunt was beginning to work up a sweat. It was still hot and humid even though the shadows had grown long and thin. However uncomfortable the temperature, though, he never minded doing hard labor for the uncle who'd taken him and his younger brothers in when they were kids. After his mother had gone into the hospital and never come out, they'd had no one else.

To one side of the carriage house was Uncle Mike's historic farmhouse, the birthplace of the town founder, Roy "Rusty" Harper's wife, Laura. Behind the house was an old red barn with stalls for his six horses, including Old Blue, and an office where Mike's wife—and Hunt's aunt—Rita, ran the Crenshaw's Moonlight Carriage Rides business. Mike and Rita depended on Hunt and his brothers to give them a hand over holidays— and when they had a moment here and there—as they couldn't afford the full-time help, now that their own three children were in college.

Today, however, it was guilt that had Hunt slaving over the chrome on the number three carriage.

"Really, Mike. C'mon. Don't claim this on your insurance. It'll send the rates through the roof. It was my fault."

Uncle Mike grunted. "Nah. These things happen. Had a few accidents of my own over the years."

"None that involved Carolina Brubaker, I'll bet," Hunt muttered.

"I gotta meet this gal. She sounds like a real spitfire."

"She's a spoiled brat. You'd be a helluva lot safer to keep your distance."

"Ya know—" Uncle Mike squinted off into the past, and his hands slowed "—the way you talk about her kinda puts me to mind of the time Rita and her best friend, Becky, got into a hair-pulling match over me, back when we were in high school."

"Aunt Rita? *My* aunt Rita? The pacifist? The woman who carries spiders outside so she doesn't have to kill them?"

Uncle Mike stopped rubbing the carriage's fender for a moment and grinned. "Yup."

Hunt glanced up at his uncle. "They were fighting over you? Shewee, dude. You musta been somethin' purty."

"Yeah, well it ain't what you think. I'd asked Rita to the prom but she said no." Mike shrugged. "I had a feeling she would. Figured since she was a Morton— of the Morton Department Store fame—that she was too good for me, the son of a simple farmer."

Hunt smiled at that. Morton's was a glorified dime-store with an old-fashioned soda fountain.

"Seemed that we were in agreement on that opinion."

Chuckling, Uncle Mike reached into his shirt pocket for a toothpick and gave the end a thoughtful chew. "Her best friend called her a snob—which was true enough—and that started the brawl. I pulled 'em apart, thanked Becky for her support and told Rita I'd pick her up at seven on Saturday."

"She thought she was too good for you, and you wanted to go out with her anyway?"

"Yep."

"Why?" His upper lip kinked, Hunt stared at his uncle.

"Well, even though she was a pain in the neck, I couldn't seem to stop thinking about her. Wonderin' what it'd be like to kiss her and such. Come to find out—the night of the prom, as luck would have it—the kisses were worth it." Uncle Mike grinned at the memory. "Seemed she was in agreement on that, too. We were married less than two years later."

"Yeah, well, we'll need snow tires in hell before that would happen in this case."

"I don't know. Weirder things have happened." Uncle Mike rubbed his sweating brow on his shirtsleeve and said, "You'd probably like Carolina, if you spent any time with her."

"Had lunch with her yesterday. Positive now. Can't stand her."

"Fine line between love and hate."

"I suppose from outer space, the Grand Canyon would be a fine line, so sure, I'll concede your point. And she's clearly from outer space."

Mike chuckled.

Hunt redoubled his efforts. Learning to like Carolina Brubaker. Ha. The very idea was ludicrous. Jaw grim, biceps bulging, he rubbed at a patch of tar stuck to the right rear fender. The two of them? Getting along? Absurd. No woman—especially some fancy-schmancy Brubaker—treated him like a second-class citizen and remained on his list of star attractions. Uncle Mike must not have had much self-esteem back then or something.

Hunt was cut from a different cloth. He had his pride.

And anyway, Aunt Rita was sane. Carolina Brubaker, on the other hand, was certifiable.

"I'm tellin' ya, Mike, the woman went completely berserk. I can understand why that McGraw character cut his losses and bolted. Though," he said, brows raised, "I'll be damned if I can figure out why he'd want to date her sister and risk ending up with Carolina as his bitter sister-in-law."

With a sigh of confusion, Hunt pushed himself away from the carriage. He stripped off his T-shirt, wadded it and mopped his face. "You ever notice that all rich people are weird?" He grinned over the shirt he held in his hands, "With the exception of Aunt Rita, of course."

"I don't know," Uncle Mike mused. "Your aunt Rita is weird enough. But I love her, anyway."

A week and a half after the fourth, the day of the hearing had finally arrived. Monday had never been Carolina's favorite day of the week. Especially at this obscene hour. Over her yawns of protest, she could hear yonder rooster heralding the sun's arrival.

Big Daddy had invited both Carolina and Hunt to meet him in his kitchen for some breakfast and a few last-minute instructions on the hearing. She glanced at the clock. Blast. Time to get up. Thrusting her covers back, she stumbled out of bed and into the shower, all the while dreading the inevitable moment when she would have to face Hunt once again. Having to go to court was bad enough, but having to go with him?

Never had she met a person who was such a burr under her saddle.

An hour later, as Carolina entered the vast stainless-steel-and-marble miracle that was the Brubaker culinary hub, she was relieved to see that, aside from Cook, she was the first to arrive. The aroma of fresh-perked java and cinnamon spiced the air. Sunlight, streaming through the floor-to-ceiling windows, filled the massive room with a cozy cheer.

A little peace and quiet to begin the day was just what the doctor ordered. Carolina headed for the coffeepot and poured herself a cup, then mixed in sugar and cream and ruminated about what she might do this afternoon, after the hearing was over and she was set free.

She hadn't been out shopping in a while. As long as she was going to be in Hidden Valley, she might just spend a little time in some of the trendy boutiques. Or maybe she'd take herself out to lunch to celebrate her victory. Then again, she studied her nails, a manicure and a massage were due. She'd tell Big Daddy that she'd take her own car into town. No use making him wait while she pampered herself.

Carolina stepped to the refrigerator to put away the cream and caught her reflection in the massive door. Leaning forward, she corrected her deep-rose-colored lipstick with a fingertip, and then inspected the rest of the package. She'd chosen a white linen pantsuit that she felt made her look both professional and, at the same time, innocent. She wore her hair upswept and fastened neatly at the back of her head with a simple gold clip. Aside from her colorful lipstick, she kept her makeup simple and professional and her scent, light. She'd given this day a lot of thought. Spent time preparing.

Practicing.

Reciting the serenity prayer.

Talking to herself about checking her temper where Hunt was concerned. She could do this. If she played her cards right, maybe she'd just get a little slap on the wrist. A warning. She lifted and dropped a shoulder. A small fine at the most. After all, the entire mess was just one big accident. Not even entirely her fault.

She issued a tiny snort.

Gracious. Putting her under arrest certainly hadn't been necessary. For heaven's sake, she was a model citizen. This was all just a huge mistake. Would all be forgotten by this time next week.

With a stifled yawn, she shut the refrigerator and brought her mug to her lips.

She'd talked to Big Daddy about hiring a lawyer, but he'd advised against it, saying he'd already spoken to the judge and had a feeling that everything would turn out just the way it was supposed to. Carolina blew across her coffee, sending ripples and steam rolling. Undoubtedly, her uncle knew what was best.

Her sigh fogged the surface of the refrigerator and as the mist slowly receded, Carolina could see Hunt's fuzzy reflection coming in through the back door. In the morning hush of the kitchen, she could suddenly hear her heart beating. With wary eyes, she watched him spot her. He stopped dead in his tracks, removed his Stetson, plunged a hand through his hair and then clapped his hat back into place.

Carolina bristled. Clearly, the man had no manners when it came to standing in the presence of a lady. Slowly she turned to face him.

"Coffee's fresh. There's a mug for you next to the machine."

"Thanks."

Good. Pleasantries over. Now she could ignore him.

She strolled over to the windows and allowed her gaze to rove toward the stables and the paddock beyond. Wait a second. What was that? Her focus returned to the stable. She frowned. Taking several steps closer to the window, she peered out into the stable's guest parking area.

Odd.

That looked just like Brandon's rig parked in front of the stable. Her eyes scanned the license plate. It *was* Brandon's rig! What on earth was *he* doing here? And at this time of the morning? Had he come to apologize? To make up with her and beg her forgiveness for being such a cad? Would she accept his apology this morning? Or should she make him grovel a bit and then soften? She favored making him grovel. After all, he'd embarrassed her to no end over that Georgia thing.

Hunt noticed the direction of her gaze and grinned. "Your boyfriend's here for a horsy ride. I just saddled his mount."

"He is?" Forgetting her vow to ignore Hunt, Carolina gaped at the stables. Brandon wanted to take her for a ride? If that was the case, why hadn't he called to make sure she'd be available? "Why didn't you tell him I had to go to court this morning?"

"Well, apparently he had a hankering to take your sister Georgia for a ride instead."

Carolina blanched and her heart leaped to her throat. "Georgia's out there?"

"Yup. Saddled her mount, too."

"You're lying." Heart flailing like a hay thrasher, Carolina spun to face Hunt. "Just to get my blood boiling before the hearing."

With a shrug Hunt moved to the coffeepot and helped himself. "Believe what you want." He took a seat at the island and shuffled through the paper till he found the sports section and then buried his nose.

Carolina spun back to the window and strained to see who would appear in the paddock. Surely Georgia would never betray her in such a manner. There was no way that…she'd… Carolina cupped her hands at the sides of her face and squinted into the distance.

Brandon was emerging from the stable, leading the horse Hunt had saddled for him. Behind Brandon—Carolina's mouth went dry, her face red and her stomach, south—was Georgia. And she was leading a horse.

Carolina clutched the window moldings to keep from slipping to her knees. No. She shook her head. This simply could not be happening. Not today. And certainly not in front of Hunt. She took a deep, calming breath and told herself not to overreact. After all, she didn't know all of the facts, and it only *appeared* that Georgia was a double-crossing slime toad, when in fact…in fact…

Okay. Carolina needed the facts. And she needed them now. "Tell Big Daddy that I'll meet him in here in a little while. I have to go to the stable for a minute to take care of some personal business."

Before she could make it to the kitchen's back door, Hunt had beaten her there and was blocking the way out.

"You're not serious."

She affected a breezy stance. Difficult, considering she felt like fainting. "About what?"

"About going to the stable and making a fool of yourself."

"I don't know what you're talking about."

"I'm talking about replaying the little scene from the Fourth. And this time dragging your sister down with you."

"I simply want to say hello."

Hunt guffawed. "*Hello?* Right. And after that? Die scum, die?"

"Don't be absurd." She pushed against his chest with her palm, but it was like trying to move a brick outhouse. "If you'll excuse me?"

"No. I won't. Big Daddy told us to be here now, and here we stay. I want to get to court, get it over with and get back to work. You're staying put."

Carolina gasped. "Where do you get off telling me where I can, and cannot go? It is my *perfect right* to go visit with my sister, if that's what I want."

"If your sister wanted to see you, she would have made a point of having you meet her there. Now, back off."

"I'll…uff," she grunted as she attempted to muscle her way by Hunt, "I will do no such thing!"

But Hunt would have no part of waiting for her to throw a tantrum. She was here, and she was going to stay here.

"Let me go!" Carolina squealed as she squeezed between Hunt's arm and the doorknob. He rolled to his side, effectively pinning her arm. "Oww! You're hurting me."

"Then stay put. You have an appointment at court, and you will not be late."

"Watch me, you big jerk."

Arms flailing, feet kicking, Carolina was lifted, without ceremony, into the air and tossed over Hunt's shoulder.

After taking a split second to survey the premises, Hunt decided the pantry would make a nice holding tank and strode across the floor. Cook watched with a befuddled expression. He knew Hunt well enough to know that he'd never hurt the boss's niece. And he also knew Carolina well enough to know that a little time in the pantry couldn't exactly hurt. So, no one rushed to her aid.

"*Helllllpppp! Someone, please! Help* me!" Carolina pounded Hunt between the shoulder blades as he stepped into the pantry and kicked the door shut. "What the hell do you think you are *doing?*" She blinked in the semidarkness.

"I'm—" Hunt was panting now, from the exertion "—keeping you from making a huge mistake." He set her on her feet and, reaching behind him, fumbled until he found the double-key bolt lock that was only used at night and only after Cook had retired for the evening.

"I demand that you let me out of here at once!"

"No!" After he locked the door, he pulled her groping hands off his face and captured her wrists. "*I* demand that you leave your sister alone and go to court so that we can put this whole thing behind us."

"You don't have a clue what I want to discuss with my sister, and besides, it's none of your damned business," she spat, her furious breath warming the flesh of his neck.

"You made it my business when you dragged me—and my horse—into your three-ring circus last week. Just let the man date whoever he wants."

"He doesn't know who he wants. That's the problem. He wants *everyone* in our family."

"Not you. He made that perfectly clear. And your older sister is married. So, let 'em be."

"I don't want him hurting Georgia."

"Georgia is a big girl. She can take care of herself."

Beyond the pantry door, the sound of Big Daddy's jovial voice as he greeted Cook reverberated throughout the room.

"Let me go. Now." Carolina's whisper was furious. "Or I'll scream so loud your mama will go deaf."

"Just try it," Hunt said and, crushing her mouth under his own, proceeded to shut her up the only way he knew how.

Chapter Five

Dazed, Carolina groped behind her back for a shelf to give some support and only succeeded in knocking over a stack of soup cans.

"Shh." Hunt steered her further into the pantry. "Big Daddy might hear us."

Before she could respond, he'd reclaimed her lips, rendering her wordless once again. Wordless but not silent. Little mewling sounds built in her throat and her breathing was so heavy, she was sure it was audible to the entire kitchen. Now and again, she would gasp, both from Hunt's bold assault on her neck and from her idiotically wanton response to this—she grimaced—this creep.

She had to remind herself just whom she was dealing with here. Hunter Crenshaw was arrogance personified. Just a big…mean…cowboy. She oughta be slapping his face. Hard. And she would, too, if she could just remember what she'd done with her hands.

The audacity. The unmitigated…gall.

Up over the fine linen that hugged the swell of her

hips, he ran his palms, and from there he moved them to her back, her shoulders and finally to her face. The difference between his gentle touch and his work-roughened hands was incredibly sexy as he cupped her face and urged her lips more firmly beneath his.

Oh, the exquisiteness of it all. Her lids were so heavy. Her body so limp. Her extremities so tingly. She lolled back against a stack of fifty-pound flour bags that filled one closet corner and wondered at the sensations going on in her body.

Why was she allowing this?

Because she couldn't think, that's why. In fact, she could barely breath. Lack of oxygen to the brain could make one do…things…they wouldn't ordinarily…do. Hands filled with his hair, she tugged his head ever closer, even as her lips were fused with his. Even as they breathed in unison. Even as their hearts pounded, one against the other.

Carolina's knees were wobbling. Her entire body, thrumming.

Certainly, *he* didn't seem to be suffering from the wet noodle syndrome that had assailed her. His biceps were steely and his chest, a curvy slab of marble. Like a blasted caveman, he knew what he wanted, clubbed it over the head and dragged it to his cave, without a single second thought.

And, though she was loath to admit it, it was wonderful.

The sounds of voices outside the pantry urged her to try to regain her sanity. But even as she knew she had to get away in order to think clearly, she merely found herself clutching him closer.

They kissed as though it was the end of the world, but for the life of her, Carolina couldn't figure out why, given the fact that they'd never shared a civil word.

Moaning, she wound an ankle around his stiff denim-clad leg and wedged herself more firmly into his embrace.

Oooh. She hated him. With every fiber of her being, she detested him. Why then, was she kissing him as if he was a long-lost lover? In all her life, she'd never behaved this way with a man. In fact, she'd only shared a few sedate kisses with Brandon in the weeks they'd dated.

She was floating. Leaden. Her body was on fire. On ice. Hot. Cold. Shivery. Molten. He kissed her neck. No, he devoured her neck. And she loved it. Goose bumps were drag-racing from arm to arm, from leg to leg. They were both panting like a pair of coal billows, fanning the flames.

They froze when they heard Big Daddy's voice right outside the pantry.

"Cook, have you seen my niece Carolina yet this fine mornin'?"

Breathing as quietly as humanly possible, given the circumstances, Carolina and Hunt remained motionless, nose-to-nose, lower lips a hair's breadth apart, foreheads together.

"That coffee and cinnamon buns I smell?" Luckily, Big Daddy was easily distracted by fine pastry. "I imagine I'll just help myself to one of them big ones 'at just came outta the oven there, Cookie."

"And I'll get you a plate," Cook said.

"Truly, I have the finest staff this side of the Mississippi." Big Daddy replied.

As she clutched Hunt's shirt, Carolina began to regain her senses. "What are we going to do now?" As she peered through the frosted glass of the pantry door, her whisper became high and tinny. "For crying out loud, he's sitting out there, eating!"

Hunt bent to squint with Carolina. "Settle down grasshopper, it's not the end of the world."

"Not for you, you big clod. He's not your uncle. He thinks I'm as pure as the driven snow."

"Yeah. Till you drifted." The old line pushed a lop-sided grin into Hunt's lips.

"I really should slap you silly. I'll have you know that I have never, ever done this…this…*stuff* with anyone before."

"You mean this stuff?" Turning her around, and pressing her back into the flour sacks, Hunt consumed her mouth and, once again, she was lost in the sensation.

Her head dropped back on her shoulders, and when he finally released her, she exhaled a groan of disgust with herself. "Yes, *that* stuff."

"You expect me to believe that? The way you kiss?"

"Yes, I expect you to believe that. My daddy would kill me for acting this way. And so will Big Daddy when he catches us. He'll probably fire you."

"And he'll probably send you home."

"Cook!" Big Daddy's voice commanded the attention of all in the next room. "My niece come down here and talk to you yet this morning?"

"Uhh…this morning?" Cook hedged.

"We have to go out there sometime," Carolina said, and with the clammy flats of her hands, smoothed her white linen suit.

"Yeah. Okay." Hunt straightened her collar and tucked her hair back behind her ears.

"So. What's our story?"

"Cook needed some…some…some…" Hunt snagged a box in the dark and without further ado, threw open the door. "Wheaties! Here you go, Cook! We looked and looked and you *do* have Wheaties!"

Puzzled, Cook nodded and glanced at Big Daddy. "Wheaties." He thrust them out at Big Daddy. "The breakfast of champions."

"Why thank you, Cook, but—" Big Daddy burped, tugged his bib from around his neck, took one last slurp of coffee and said, "Now that we're all here, we've gotta fly. The courthouse is expectin' us."

Hunt strolled toward the back door and tried to look uninterested. Bored. Certainly not as if he was dying to jump back into the closet for another quick go-round.

With Carolina Brubaker.

What on earth just happened there? Had to be tension. Yeah. That was it. The tension of having to go to court. Hunt removed his hat and adjusted its brim. What else could have possessed him?

He dragged a hand over his mouth. It would take an hour at least for his blood pressure to return to normal. Let alone his other bodily functions. He was positively vibrating with excitement. He glanced at Carolina and wondered what was going on in her head.

She was standing there, gaping into a compact, scrubbing at her mouth and applying fresh lipstick.

Cool as a cucumber all right.

He bit his upper lip to forestall a sneer of self-disgust. Here he was, panting like a blasted bull eyeing the swirling red cape, and there she was, calmly removing all traces of him from her face.

She snapped her compact shut and stalked past him. "Don't ever try that again."

"No problem." Once more, he chalked his momentary attraction up to the insanity of the moment. Time to drop the whole episode from his memory base. Obviously, she had.

As they entered the Hidden Valley Senior Center, Carolina could feel Hunt's gaze upon her every move. She dared not glance at him for fear he would read something in her eyes that would give away how their little tryst in the pantry had affected her. The rapid click-ing of her heels echoed across the lobby's checkered li-noleum in rhythm with her racing heart. All the fluorescent lights in the room had rainbow halos and ev-erything seemed to have a sort of "glowy" quality. Even the floor seemed to be tilting at odd angles. Feeling as dazed and unsteady as she did, it was all Carolina could do to follow Big Daddy and concentrate on what he was saying.

"Since we don't have enough room in the court-house, the senior center has graciously consented to let the county hold the various public legal meetin's here until next year's budget passes. It's crude, sure, but it serves the purpose for now. Hey, Milton. Harvey."

Big Daddy gestured to a couple of octogenarians and told Carolina as they moved through the room, "Harvey's the retired postmaster, went to school with my Miss Clarise's daddy, and though he's nearly ninety, Milton over there leads the AA meetin's here on Friday nights and the swimrobics classes on Saturday morn-ings. Great old guys."

"Mmm—haah—mm." Carolina's response was dis-tracted as she made the monumental mistake of glanc-ing at Hunt.

His jeans fit as snugly as an old lady's best Sunday shoes, and his narrow hips rocked like Elvis on a roll as he strolled down the hall. He moved with a natural masculinity that had the blue-haired girls behind the lobby desk twittering after him and then hoo-hooing and hee-hawing about how that youngster could park his boots under their bed anyday.

Carolina frowned. How had his phenomenally good looks escaped her notice before that very mo-ment? Perhaps it was the permanent scowl he wore whenever he deigned to rest his gaze on her. In any event, he was clearly a head turner, no matter what the age.

The teensiest, weensiest—completely crazy—feeling of rogue jealousy stabbed into the irrational side of her brain. Sparked, no doubt, by that clandestine kiss in the pantry that morning. Luckily, the rational side of her brain still hated Hunt's rippling Zeus-like guts and so, with a deep breath, she blew the lunacy away.

Once they'd reached the check-in desk, handed over their citations and had been directed down the hall and to the left by Selma Featherstone, they entered the makeshift hearing room.

Carolina blinked around the bright space and tried like mad to orient herself. According to the handwritten banner that was stretched across the back wall, today was Traffic Violation Day. The lighted bingo board had been unplugged and settled in the corner with the rest of the usual Saturday-night entertainment paraphernalia: a slide projector, scrabble tournament tables and a bucket full of neon swim noodles.

A card table was set up near the back wall for Judge Scruggs's use, and a podium stood in the middle of the room for the convenience of the offender. Chairs were situated in theater-style rows for those who waited.

Over by the exit door, Officer Scruggs stood, legs spread and hands folded behind his rigid back, jaw jutting with authority. As Carolina stepped to the row of chairs her uncle had selected, Officer Scruggs peered over the top of his expensive sunglasses, and the tiniest hint of a smile flirted with his stony expression.

Eager to rekindle their fledgling friendship—especially should she need an ally during her testimony today—Carolina returned his smile and fluttered her fingertips. Thankfully, it seemed as if Officer Scruggs had forgiven her little gender mishap. She offered a wordless "hi."

He nodded.

Gesturing with her hands beneath her breasts, she mouthed in a confidential manner, "They're fine."

Several old-timers, including Harvey and Milton, from the senior center gang—most of whom came to watch the legal proceedings because it was better than daytime TV—exchanged interested glances under the arches of their woolly brows. They seemed to wonder, could young Eustace finally be getting some action? Hoary heads bent forward as they canoodled among themselves and wheezed with laughter.

Officer Scruggs's gaze dropped to the bustline in question. He gave his head an official bob and then resumed his stance.

Hunt's deep-throated groan of disgust pretty much summed up his feelings on their chummy byplay. Carolina shot him a withering look as she squeezed past him and shuffled down the row of folding chairs to claim a spot next to Big Daddy. Upon settling into her slightly bent and rocking, icy cold chair, she took a moment to pop a breath mint and rub a bit of scented lotion on her hands.

Hunt dropped into the seat next to her and without ceremony held out a pack of gum.

She sent him a glance meant to shrivel. As if. She grabbed the whole pack and shoved it into her purse.

"Hey," he protested.

"Do without your damned cud for a simple hour, okay? We're in a professional setting."

"That why you were showing your 'mammos' off to Officer Scruggs?"

She ground her back teeth so hard it was a wonder her fillings weren't bursting forth like so much bomb shrapnel. "Shut up. Shut up. Shut. *Up.*"

"Very professional."

"Shut up."

Judge Scruggs, lugging an armful of files and still struggling to don his black satin robe, rushed into the room and signaled for Selma to bring him a cup of coffee.

"All rise and salute the flag," young Officer Scruggs instructed the motley, and still mostly asleep, traffic violation crowd. Off to the far side of the room, the senior center peanut gallery dragged off their fishing caps and fumbled to find their hearts.

In a somewhat scattered unison, traffic offenders of all shapes and sizes uttered the age-old words of allegiance to the stars and stripes that hung from a pole in the corner by the TV. When silence had rung for a good beat after "for all," Judge Scruggs instructed "all" to take a seat and wait until their name was called. He zipped up his robe and gave his scalding coffee some tongue-blistering sips.

Someone in Harvey and Milton's group cracked a joke, and there was a bit of cackling until the judge silenced them with a narrow glance.

As the judge shuffled through the pile of tickets and other miscellaneous paper work, Hunt was chagrined to find himself once again at the mercy of Officer "Dragnet" Scruggs's father. He ducked his head low and hoped to remain incognito.

This was not good. Old Man Scruggs was a deceptively mild-mannered guy who had not taken kindly to Hunt's treatment of his son, back in grade school. More than one of his weekends had been spent mowing the judge's lawn while junior shot at him with his infernal rubber band gun. Yessiree. This was gonna be a long day.

After what seemed like endless waiting for the judge to ponder Edith Bunson and Cora Sellburn's fender-bender down at the Park 'N' Snack, and Frankie Monroe's muffler-and-rap noise-pollution dilemmas, Carolina and Hunt were finally summoned to the podium. The judge took a minute to read the list of infractions, while Milton and Harvey and the gang ooh'd and ahh'd over the unusual case and hobnobbed in a huddle.

The judge pushed his heavy glasses high on his nose and peered at Hunt. "Son, don't I know you?"

Hunt grimaced and glanced at Junior. "I went to Hidden Valley Elementary with your son, sir."

"Ah." That seemed to explain a boatload to the judge. He nodded first at Hunt, then at Carolina. "How do you plead?"

"Not guilty," Carolina stated in a firm voice.

"Guilty," Hunt said simultaneously.

"*What?*" Together, their heads snapped round and they stared at each other. Hunt was the first to find his voice. "*Not* guilty? Are you kidding? If anyone is guilty in the fiasco, it's *you!*"

"There would have been no problem at all, if you had simply followed the cab as I requested!" Carolina stated, hands on her hips.

"You call beating the crap out of my horse a *request?*"

"Oh, for crying in the night. A sting with a riding crop had nothing to do with your nag's need for a diaper."

Hunt lifted the podium and slammed it back on the linoleum, effectively capturing everyone's—including the hall janitor's—rapt attention. "Listen, lady—"

"No, *you* listen up, buster—" Frustrated, Carolina grabbed the podium and they began to rock it back and forth in a ridiculous struggle for power.

The judge's gavel rang out like a shot, causing the

entire room to gasp and freeze. "Both of you listen to *me*."

With a slow creak and a groan, the bottom dropped off the podium and crashed to the floor, leaving the wedge-shaped top suspended between their hands. A ripple of laughter rumbled through the audience. Milton chortled, and Yoo-hoo sprayed from Harvey's large nostrils. Hunt and Carolina dared not move, and awkwardly held the tabletop balanced between them. Fearing the judge's wrath, they stood frozen and attempted to act as if nothing were amiss.

In the ensuing silence, the judge scribbled copious notes. He licked his fingers, turned a page and scribbled some more. After it seemed to Carolina that he could have penned his life story, His Honor set down his pen and removed his glasses. He rubbed his eyes for a bit, then gnawed the stem of his specs. Everyone sat spellbound. The ticktock of the clock on the wall seemed magnified. It was clear that there hadn't been this much excitement in Hidden Valley in quite some time.

Judge Scruggs opened his mouth to speak, and everyone surged forward. In a placid yet no-nonsense voice, he addressed the two standing at what was left of the podium.

"I do not like what I am seeing in either of you."

Both Hunt and Carolina hung their heads.

"Seems to me, your attitudes could use some serious adjustment. So—" he donned his glasses and peered through the huge lenses "—I'll accept both of your pleas as guilty. I believe that's what I heard you both say?"

Carolina opened her mouth, then snapped it shut.

"If you are ready, I am prepared to mete out your punishment."

Both Hunt and Carolina gave contrite, barely discernible nods.

"Community service."

Carolina flagged with relief as a perky smile filled up her face and lit her eyes. "Great! Can do. Just let me know where the service is to be held, and I'll be there, with bells on."

Her smile faded at Hunt's rancorous glance.

"What?" She glanced about. Why was everyone in the room looking at her so strangely? She'd been nothing if not chipper and cooperative. "What?"

The judge fingered his turkey-gobbler neck as he regarded Carolina. "Young woman, for your information, community service is not a one-time occasion. In fact, for you—and your cohort in crime there—" the judge nodded in Hunt's direction "—I am prescribing a series of services that you will perform for the community in order to make reparations and amends. So, how fast you work will determine how many weeks you will be serving the community."

Carolina's jaw fell slack. "Weeks?"

"Perhaps months."

"*Months!* Why, that is simply impossible!" She flung her fabulous hair over her shoulder and offered one of her breathtaking smiles. "I am not an official resident of this lovely town."

Old Dragnet lowered his sunglasses and all but salivated, Hunt noted in irritation. He only hoped Judge Scruggs was oblivious to her rather considerable charms.

"And, as much as I'd love to help out, I simply will not be able to join in on the community services. I'm sure my family will support me in this." She dug through her purse and withdrew a fist full of credit cards. "Where do I make my donation? I'll be happy to provide refreshments."

"We'll come to fines in a moment. For now let's discuss your community service." Before she could form a protest, the judge continued. "First off, I have decided that you will attend anger management classes up in East Central Dallas—"

"Anger management?" Carolina's laughter tinkled at that. "Really. You have *got* to be *kidding*. Seriously now. I was voted Miss Congeniality two years running in the Dairyman's Beauty Pageant." She turned and smiled at the audience.

Congenial? Hunt frowned. How was that possible?

Her announcement made no impression on the judge, who continued. "Every Monday evening for eight weeks in a row."

"Eight weeks?"

The judge continued without so much as a glance at Carolina's high-pitched squeal. "Upon completion of said course, the courts will receive a certificate that will be attached to your permanent records. As luck would have it, the next session begins tonight."

"Tonight?" Again Carolina glanced in appeal at Big Daddy who could only shrug and feign shock.

"See Clerk Selma Featherstone for directions to the campus." The judge shuffled his fistful of papers. "Furthermore, your public service duties will commence this very morning." The judge did not look up and only the most astute reader of body language could tell that the man was delighting in this particular announcement. "Your first assignment will be to clean the streets of litter."

"What? *Clean the streets?*" Carolina blanched. "*This* morning?" She gestured to her snow-white pantsuit. "I can't muck the ditches in this outfit!"

"You will be provided with a standard county-issue jumpsuit, complete with safety vest and head gear to wear during your course of labor. These services, to be performed every Monday, will take roughly five work-ing days for the greater Hidden Valley area, not includ-ing the fairgrounds, which I'm guesstimating will take the better part of a week in and of itself.

"Wh…wha…" Carolina slumped against the top of the podium, causing Hunt to stagger under the added weight. Her face was covered with a cold sheen of de-spair.

"When the cleaning has been completed, the county sign shop will assist you in the repair of all signs. We'll have you consult with private contractors for advice on the fences and other public property broken by the car-riage."

Carolina swallowed and blinked. What the devil was this madman saying? She had to *fix* all this stuff? She hadn't a clue how to do any of this…this…*labor.* The men in her family treated the women as rare flowers. Brubaker women didn't have to touch tools or lift heavy things, or even break a sweat if a personal trainer wasn't involved.

"Because I believe in contrition, both written and ver-bal, I'm going to require you to personally apologize to the victims and perform helpful tasks for one day per person." The judge shuffled his papers. "I have spoken to the victims, and services such as baby-sitting, cook-ing, cleaning, dog walking and more are needed. These tasks will be allotted a two-week period to accomplish in their entirety. And finally your services will end over at the widow Foster's place, where you will work at landscaping, porch repair and rebuilding the screen door."

Carolina swayed with the podium top and wondered in a dazed fashion, that if this was *her* punishment, what in the world did the judge have in store for— Hunt's profile wavered before her—*him?* Thumb screws? The gallows? Water torture? Even these imaginative thoughts failed to cheer her.

The judge continued. "There will be a number of knickknacks and sundries that need gluing and replacement, including that podium you hold there, Mr. Crenshaw. My son, Officer Scruggs, will be overseeing your duties this summer. You will report to him each morning, and he will check up on you, to make sure that you are each busy performing your civic duties. Is that clear?"

Wordlessly Carolina nodded, though she had no clue as to the question.

"Good." The smack of the judge's gavel echoed throughout the room. "Any questions? Yes, Ms. Brubaker?"

"Uh, yes, Your Excellency. I was just wondering what 'services' to the community you have in mind for him?" Like Vanna at the letter board, Carolina stepped aside and gestured to Hunt.

The judge adjusted his glasses and frowned. "Apparently I did not make myself clear. You will *both* be doing all of the aforementioned duties. Together."

"To…*gether?*" They both gaped at the judge in horror.

"Together?" With a collective gasp, the peanut gallery hunched forward to better hear. "Those two?"

The room was fairly vibrating.

"Yes." The judge nodded. "Together. You'll be performing all community services *together* until you have completed your assigned hours. Since y'all can't seem to get along, you'll have plenty of time to practice what you'll be learning in anger management class.

"So, to review." In a monotone, the judge reiterated, ticking off one finger at a time. "You will ride out to the work location *together.* You will work all day long at your assigned task *together.* You will take your lunch breaks *together.* You will get along *together.* And when the day is over, you will ride home to the Circle BO...*together.* That clear?"

"You want me to work with *her?* For the next *two months?*" The top half of the podium thudded to the floor. "How the hell are we supposed to get anything done?"

"I guess that's for you two to figure out. Together." The judge stood. "Officer Scruggs will escort you both to the changing area. From there you will begin your duties. Good luck."

Chapter Six

Later that same morning—after they'd been given some time to change into county-issue jumpsuits, complete with orange safety vests—Hunt and Carolina were directed to wait on the courthouse porch until Officer Scruggs arrived to give them their first assignment. As Hunt held the front door open for Carolina, a searing blast of Texas heat nearly drove him back to request the merely sweltering discomfort of a jail cell.

Hell's bells, it was hot.

He paused as she strode past, her orange vest slung over her shoulder by a fingertip. With a resigned sigh, he followed her outside. If the delicate Carolina Brubaker could take the heat, so could he.

Together they waited in silence. By the rigid set of her posture, as she leaned against a porch post and scowled at her chunky work boots, Hunt could tell Carolina wasn't in the mood for polite chitchat.

Suited him just fine.

Settling onto a wooden bench in the shade, he

squinted after a distant tractor and watched it kick up a funnel of dust as it plowed a field. There wasn't a single cloud on the horizon in all directions. The windsock on the roof of radio station WBHV just lay there, limp in the heat. The time/temp sign over the Hidden Valley Savings and Loan flashed one hundred degrees and rising and it was nowhere near noon. Under a shade tree, an ancient hound gave his tail a languid thump to keep the flies away.

Oh, yeah. It was gonna be a scorcher. Killer. Hunt swiped at his forehead with the sleeve of his jumpsuit. Already a small river of sweat trickled between his shoulder blades and began to pool at the elastic waistband of his underwear. In Texas, July was rarely ever a breeze, even on a shady porch here in town. But out on a long stretch of prairie asphalt? He could only imagine the shimmering afternoon sun. On the road. With no shade.

With her.

He shifted his gaze.

Even in the ugly blue jumpsuit, Carolina managed to look cool and trendy. Chic. She'd rolled up the sleeves and pushed them above her elbows. A jaunty ponytail tickled her shoulders and, at her crown, an expensive pair of fashionable sunglasses perched like a tiara. She looked as cool as the other side of the pillow.

Apparently, her ilk didn't go in for sweating.

Dragging a hand over his upper lip, Hunt rubbed at the smirk he was afraid was becoming a permanent fixture. Great. Just great. He was doing time with one of the Gabor sisters. Already, he could envision the 911 calls to the manicurist.

After another ten silent, sweltering minutes in the shade, Officer Scruggs finally burst through the doors and joined them on the porch. Making them wait out here in the heat showed who was in control, Hunt guessed. It also gave Scruggs that chance to gussy up a tad. As the officer moved to meet with them, the smell of his cloying aftershave hung in the stagnant air.

"You two ready to get started?"

"Mmm." Tilting her head at a coquettish angle, Carolina bestowed Scruggs with a flattering smile. "Somebody smells wonderful."

"Oh." A rashy stain crawled up Scruggs's neck and settled in his cheeks. It was clear, as he fumbled with his clipboard, that he was suddenly having trouble focusing on his mission.

"Uh, okay your truck is parked, uh, over here, behind the station. It's brand-new. Loaded. So—" turning his back on Hunt, Scruggs issued a beet-red chuckle to Carolina "—be careful. You'll be the first to use it—"

As Carolina sidled up to Scruggs's arm and batted her baby blues, the rash spread from his cheeks to his forehead and the tips of his ears.

The officer swallowed, cleared his throat and then gestured for them to follow him around the building to the gleaming rig that appeared to have come off the showroom floor that morning. There was a brand-new county sticker on the door.

"The map and site instructions are in the glove compartment. Selma loaded a lunch into a cooler since you didn't have time to go home. In the back of the truck you'll find all the supplies you'll need—water, orange cones, hard hats, traffic signs, safety gear, trash bags…" He tightened his grip on his clipboard. "Okay. After you've filled a bag with refuse, tie it off and leave it on the…the…the…"

Hunt could tell, even through the dark glasses, that Scruggs's eyes were roving over the perky cleavage shadowed beneath the zipper of Carolina's jumpsuit.

The lascivious—and thoroughly unprofessional—expression on his face negated any sympathy Hunt may have mustered for the clumsy late bloomer.

Scruggs was a creep.

And not just because he was a control freak, but because he was a scheming, ingratiating, manipulative control freak. Same as he was back in the sixth grade. Hunt cracked his knuckles. And, as he had back in the sixth grade, he battled the urge to sink his fist into Scruggs's red-veined nose. Carolina had no idea what kind of fire she was playing with there.

"…the…shoulder." Scruggs swallowed and took a deep breath. "The sanitation crew will be out later to pick them up." He held out a set of keys. "These are for your rig."

Hunt reached out and snatched the keys before they could drop into Carolina's uplifted palm. "I'll drive."

"Hey! That's not fair. Officer Scruggs wanted me to drive, didn't you, hon?"

"I…" Officer Scruggs's face grew impossibly more mottled. "I don't see why she shouldn't drive."

"Do you even have a license?" Thumbs hooked in his rear pockets, Hunt rocked back on his heels and regarded Carolina with skepticism.

"I have a perfectly good learner's permit." To Scruggs she said, "At school I really had no reason to learn to drive. My sisters drive, though. And I've been practicing with Basil all summer long."

"Driving up and down the driveway while your uncle's chauffeur naps in the back seat is hardly what I'd call getting you "road ready," Hunt said.

"*You're* the boss, Officer Scruggs." She batted her baby blues up at Scruggs, who was suddenly heady with power.

Mouth set in a thin line, he turned the twin mirrors of his sunglasses on Hunt. "She can drive."

Hunt tossed the keys to Carolina, closed his eyes and rubbed the spot between his brows that had begun to throb. Mmm-hmm.

A long, long, long damn day.

For five endless miles they lurched down a deserted stretch of highway toward the intersection where Scruggs had suggested they should start collecting garbage. By now Hunt had a numbing case of whiplash to go with his headache. Carolina didn't know the clutch from the most basic of holes in the ground and seemed unwilling to admit its necessity.

Once Scruggs had helped her get the engine started, it was hell-bent for leather in first gear, until it was time to stop at traffic signals. Sometimes, she opted not to stop, since using the stupid clutch would simply "mess her up." When they'd finally arrived at their destination, Hunt heaved a huge sigh of relief and pointed to a wide spot under a lone oak at the side of the road.

"That looks as good a place as any."

Lip curled, there was a little cluck of disgust in Carolina's heavy sigh. "Why *there?* I don't want to park at the side of the road. This is a new truck. It might get scratched."

Hunt rubbed the tightly strung chords at the back of his neck. Swinging to face her, he swallowed back a sharp retort and made an effort to play nice. "Where would you like to park?"

"Let's find a parking lot."

Deep breath. "If you will look around, you will see that we have left the greater metropolitan area of Hidden Valley. There are no 'parking lots' out here in the middle of Cockroach, Nowhere. Get it? No latte bars, no clothing boutiques, no parking lots. So stop clowning around and *park.* We have work to do."

"You don't have to be so mean." Ignoring the clutch, Carolina slammed on the brake and killed the engine. "Now look what you made me do."

"I'm sorry. Please. Just…park." Hunt exhaled and spoke as if to a child. "Over there. At the side of the road. Under that tree. Where there is some shade."

He leaned back and waited as she searched for clues as to how to restart the engine. He drummed his fingers on the dash. His watch beeped the hour. Time passed. Frustration sharpened his voice.

"Clutch. Neutral. Key. Gas."

"I *know!*"

"Just trying to help."

"Bull." Finally she started the engine, located first gear and continued crawling down the road.

Hunt stared at her, then out the window, then back at her. "Hello? We're here. This—" out the window, his arm swept the countryside "—is the place. You can stop driving now." Still, they lurched down the road. "Carolina?"

"I haven't learned to back up yet, okay?"

"Oh, for crying in the night! Here." Hunt reached over and, gripping her by the knee, jammed her foot on the clutch and, grabbing the stick, shoved the truck into reverse. "Now, ease up on the clutch, give her some gas, back up and park, okay?"

"Okay! Stop barking at me. You're making me nervous."

"*I'm* making *you* nervous?"

Hunt unzipped the front of his jumpsuit and shrugged out of the top half and let it drop to his waist. *Man.* His T-shirt was soaked. The air was humid and stifling. He was sweating like a sinner in the confessional. Though the air conditioner pumped away, it wasn't much help against the sun that blazed through the windshield.

"Now, slow down...slowly, now, because there is a very, very steep ditch on my side. *Stop!*"

Carolina jumped on the brake and tightened her already white-knuckled grip on the wheel. Since she'd killed the engine, it took her a moment to get started again.

"Now, pull out across the road. Then... *Stop!*"

Again, the engine stalled.

"Dang it, Hunt!" Exasperated, she beat on the wheel then restarted the engine. "You keep scaring the crud out of me!"

"Sorry. Okay, now, back up again." When nothing happened, he gestured to the gearbox. "Put it in reverse. Reverse." The engine was roaring, but they weren't moving. "Reverse. What are you waiting for?"

"Just quit it." She slapped his hand away. Tongue protruding past her lips in deep concentration, Carolina finally found reverse and began to back up.

Hunt suppressed a grin. Girl had pluck. Had to give her that. "Okay, that's enough. Stop. Stop. *Stop!*"

"Why? I'm fine."

"Staaaaahhhp!" Hunt stomped on his imaginary brake.

Carolina skidded to a halt, and Hunt braced for a fall. His relief was audible when they landed, rear tires a hair short of the shoulder's edge.

"Phew. That was really, really close. But—" he opened his door and peered out "—we'll be fine, *if* you put it in first and ease forward...first gear. First. *First—*"

"I can do it myself!"

"Then *do* it! And turn the wheel, or you'll—"

"Hunt, let *go!*" As she pummeled his arm with her fists, her foot slipped off the clutch and they jerked backward over a massive tree root where they suddenly found themselves high-centered, dangling, tailgate first, over the edge of the ditch. Slowly, the truck rocked back and forth on the precipice, engine whining.

"Don't move," Hunt whispered.

Confusion marred Carolina's brow. "What happened?"

"Don't even breathe."

"Why not?"

"Because we made a slight error in calculation when backing up."

"We? *We?* I wouldn't have if you—"

"Shh-hhhh-hh!"

Lips pursed, Carolina fell silent.

"Since the tree trunk is in the way on your side, you need to climb over here, onto my lap. Then, together we'll—"

"Your lap?" She issued an indelicate snort. "In your dreams, lover bo—"

"Dammit, woman! I'm not kidding! If you don't want to hurt Officer Scruggs's precious rig, listen to me."

Her expression grew serious.

"Okay. Now. Lean forward. Keep the weight toward the front of the rig. Now, very slowly, inch over toward me while I open my door—"

As instructed, Carolina unhitched her safety belt and began to work her way toward Hunt.

"Good," he murmured. "Very good. Careful now…"

The truck rocked with her every movement. Her breath came in heavy little pants as she clutched his T-shirt and stared out the rear window. "Good *heavens!* Why didn't you tell me that ditch was so *deep?*"

"Don't look. Just keep moving toward me. Come on now, I gotcha—"

Hunt slowly lifted Carolina into his lap, but all their good effort was to no avail, as the truck lost its purchase on the root, rocked wildly, then fell bed first, into the ditch.

The depressing sounds of brand-new paint being scraped off brand-new metal filled the cab. As it struck rock, the tailgate buckled, allowing the truck to jounce about in the ditch, and then, the world rolled over as it finally come to rest on its side.

Steel groaned, the engine died and steam hissed from beneath the hood.

Inside the cab, Carolina lay against Hunt, who lay against the passenger door that lay against a solid wall of rock and dirt. Though he was pretty sure he'd seriously bruised his ribs on the armrest, his first concern was for Carolina. For once in her life, she wasn't jabbering. Hurling accusations. Casting aspersions.

In fact, she wasn't moving.

At all.

Like a Raggedy Ann doll, she lay limply across his lap, her face ashen. And, as far as Hunt could tell, she wasn't breathing. Odd, considering the accident had happened so slowly, there hardly seemed the momentum for trauma.

She had to be conning him. Like he'd fall for that old routine. Man. She sure looked lifeless. Like a porcelain doll, all angelic and flawless and…white.

Too white.

In spite of the heat, gooseflesh crawled across his body. He shook her a bit, but her arms flopped at her sides like well-cooked linguine. Fingers of fear slipped into his throat and took hold.

"Carolina?"

He patted her face.

"Carolina, if you're playing some kind of stupid game to punish me, cut it out. This is not funny."

Still no response.

Okay, either she was a really, *really* good actress, intent on torturing him or she was in trouble. Big, fat, serious trouble. And here they were, out in the middle of nowhere, trapped in a sweltering hot box, just like a bad prison movie.

"Come on, woman, breathe," he urged, and unzipped her jumpsuit to her waist and loosened it around her T-shirt to give her room. Didn't seem to help much. Damn. How could anyone breathe in this wretched heat? He began to panic in earnest. "Carolina! Hey, you okay? Carolina! Answer me!"

Nothing.

With a Herculean effort, he battled back the panic and, shifting her in his lap, smoothed her hair back to better see her face. Still, pale as death. He glanced around. The only exit was Carolina's door, six feet straight up. The only flat surface available now was his door. What if she needed CPR? He could hardly give it to her with her crumpled in a ball on his lap this way.

He had to find a way out. Now.

"Carolina, if you can hear me, please say something. Anything. Something mean. Insult me. That would make you feel better, huh, honey?"

Nothing.

Hunt began to pray as he fumbled for her wrists and then her pulse.

"Lord, please, please, don't let her die. You know I don't really hate her, exactly. It's just that she's such a stubborn mule and sometimes I really want to throttle her, but not now, Lord not now please, now just let her live. And if you do, I promise I'll try to be more toler-ant and accepting and—" he winced "—forgiving, and I'll keep my mouth shut and be nice to her for the rest of the summer. Amen."

Shoulder to face, he wiped his sweat on the sleeve of his T-shirt.

Her pulse seemed to thrum beneath his fingertips.

Thump-thump. Thump-thump. Thump-thump. That much at least was comforting. Now what? Mouth-to-mouth? He vacillated. Could he hurt her if he did that? Could he hurt her if he didn't?

He should have paid more attention in high school health class.

Oh, well. No time like the present to learn.

In the crook of his elbow, he cradled her head and stroked her hair back away from her face. She was so incredibly beautiful. Her skin was as smooth as polished pearl. Her hair, like sunlight, her lashes, gossamer. Tilting her head back, he did his best to arrange a clear passageway and tipped her jaw open.

"Okay, honey. I'm gonna give you mouth-to-mouth now...."

Just before his mouth touched hers, she stirred and then inhaled deeply, filling her lungs with much-needed oxygen. "I...told you...never to do that again."

This time her tone was sardonic. Relief flooded Hunt. *Thank God!* He looked up and out the window and gave a grateful nod.

Slowly Carolina opened her eyes and blinked at her surroundings. A long, low groan built in her throat. "Ohhhh, *crap.*" Looping her arm around Hunt's neck, she pulled herself upright and promptly burst into tears.

"The *truck!*" Slumping forward, she blubbered into Hunt's T-shirt. "It's brand-*new!* Scruggs is going to *kill* me."

Hunt cocked an interested brow. She could afford to buy dozens of these trucks with mad money alone. Her brokenness was impressive. Could she be growing up? She buried her face against his T-shirt and wiped her nose and eyes.

Tucking his chin to his neck, he frowned. "Hey!"

"Sorry, but I'm dripping." She sniffed and dabbed some more. "I am never, ever going to drive again, as long as I live."

"Oh, come on, everyone has a problem on the road now and again."

"Not me. I'm through. I could have killed us."

They sighed and stared at each other for a long, unsmiling minute.

"I can't breathe," Carolina finally said.

Yeah. She was right. It was getting very close in here. For safety's sake, they needed to get out, and soon. "You feeling okay?"

She nodded. "My head aches and I think I twisted my ankle, but it's not too bad."

"Okay. In that case, how about if I give you a boost up to the driver's side window?"

There was nothing out here for miles in any direction. Without a truck, they were stuck. Glumly Carolina watched from above as Hunt stood in the ditch and surveyed the damage.

"Can you fix it?"

Hunt shrugged. "Not without an auto body shop and several mechanics. You got a cell phone?"

"I left it in my locker at the courthouse. I didn't think we'd need it."

"Groovy." He extended a hand, and Carolina helped him out of the ditch.

She was surprised by the gratitude she felt for his presence. She didn't know what she'd do, out here, in the middle of nowhere, all by herself. The very thought gave her the shivers.

"I'm going to go get help." Hunt dusted off his hands and squinted into the empty horizon. "You stay here."

"You want me to stay here? Out in the middle of nowhere? All by myself?" She stepped forward and fastened her arms around his bulging bicep. "No! Please, take me with you."

Hunt shook his head. "You're still limping."

"No I'm not."

"I can go faster by myself. I know of a farm up the road that might lend me a tractor. You stay here, in case help comes."

"But I want to go with you."

Hunt sighed. "Carolina, no. If your ankle gets worse, I can't carry you in this heat. Stay here. I'll be right back. I promise."

Lower lip between her teeth, Carolina bit back a sob. It had been a hell of a day, and it wasn't even lunchtime yet. Normally, she'd be floating around the pool at Big Daddy's place, chatting on the phone, planning a party for the weekend.

"But…" She hated how foolish she sounded. "What if there are…snakes?"

"Snakes are the least of our worries. Right now, I want to get this truck out of the ditch, turned over and running so we can get back to town."

She nodded as he set off down the road. Before he'd gone twenty paces, she felt bereft. Alone. Lonely, in fact, which was new. Carolina never felt lonely. Leaning against the trunk of the tree, she slowly slid to the ground and crossed her legs. She shaded her eyes with the edge of her hand and followed Hunt's retreating form until he became a speck on the horizon. As much as she hated to confess it, Hunt was a good man. Not only was he gorgeous, but he could do just about anything.

She picked up a handful of gravel and let it sift through her fingertips. This kind of thinking was not smart. If she wasn't careful, she was going to get sucked in by his good looks and bulging, sweaty, smooth, tanned—Carolina made a face and chucked a small rock into the middle of the road—muscles. Um, baby. He wasn't muscle-bound, by any stretch, but he was solid. Cut. Sexy. Alluring.

A vision of the kiss they'd shared in the kitchen that morning had her breath grow suddenly shallow. Oh, yeah. He'd had some practice, that much was obvious. Who were the women in his past? She'd never paid any attention before. Surely a guy who looked like him, with those smoldering eyes and those Kurt Russell lips, had to have left a trail of heartbreak in his wake.

Her tongue rimmed her lips, recalling that kiss. She wondered what mouth-to-mouth might have been like.

She had to get ahold of her thoughts. Something about him made her feel vulnerable. Since Hunt didn't even like her, getting all moony over him made no sense. Besides, there was still that whole Brandon thing to muddle through. Her eyes wandered to the mangled truck and she sighed.

Why did life have to be so hard sometimes?

Sitting back, she closed her eyes. From the neighboring wheat field came the high whine of insects. A squirrel in the branches above scolded her, warning her away. Off in the distance some cattle lowed. Carolina yawned. She was not a morning person. Aside from the golden grain, and a little grove of trees at the other end of the field, there wasn't much to look at. Nothing much to amuse her. Her eyes drifted shut.

Except dreams of Hunt.

The rumble of an engine roused Carolina from the most delicious dream. She'd been floating, floating among the fluffy clouds of wheat. Wheaties…actually. The breakfast of champions.

The rumble of the engine grew louder.

Slowly her eyes worked their way open.

She sat up.

Hunt?

Was Hunt back?

Excited, she hobbled to her feet and peered in the direction of the sound. No. Couldn't be Hunt. It was coming from the wrong end of the road. And it wasn't a tractor. It was a pickup. Music with indiscernible—yet somehow frightening—lyrics rumbled so loudly Carolina could feel the vibrations from here. Stepping behind a tree, she peeked out and saw a man driving a dilapidated flat-bed truck, loaded with junk. Something about this guy—and his buddy—had Carolina's creep radar on alert. She shivered. She was alone. Out here. In the middle of nowhere.

Spooked, she forgot her sore ankle, scooted into the ditch and crawled up to the other side where she could hide amongst the brambles at the edge of the wheat field. At least until she knew that the passersby were nicer than their throbbing, shrieking music.

Hunt. She pressed her hands to her mouth. *Hunt, hurry, hurry, hurry! Oh, where are you?*

The raging music died along with the truck's noisy diesel engine.

"Well, whadaya suppose happened here?" A man's voice rang out in the sudden, eerie silence.

"Ted, we ain't got time to stop and look at some wrecked truck."

"Yeah, but, Willie, them hubcaps is brand-new. And clearly somebody threw this rig away." The old pickup's heavy door creaked opened, then slammed shut.

"I'm tellin' ya, we ain't got time. Lonnie'll kill us if we're late."

"Not if we show up bearin' gifts."

"Lonnie don't care about no hubcaps."

"Willie boy, I'm telling ya, them tires are worth a fortune. Goodyear. Brand-new. Plus, I bet there are some goodies under the hood that still function…."

Carolina felt the panic begin to rise. They were going to steal their tires? And the goodies?

"Ted, that truck probably belongs to somebody."

"Not anymore. Finder's keepers." Footsteps crunched across the gravel. "That's my motto." The reedy laughter of a man who'd been smoking since before he was out of preschool rumbled around a stream of gleeful profanity.

Carolina's eyes slid back in her head. Her face was cold, her feet were hot and everything in between was preparing for an attack of nausea. She'd never been so afraid in her life. Covering her mouth with her hands, she stifled the scream she felt welling.

"You hear that, Willie?"

"What?"

"Sounds like something's in them bushes over there."

"Where?"

"Willie, just get my crowbar."

Chapter Seven

"What a super first day on the job, huh?" Lower lip protruding, Carolina stretched out the neck of her sleeveless T-shirt and blew. She'd long since shrugged out of the top half of her sweltering denim jumpsuit and let it dangle from her waist. "We haven't picked up one single piece of garbage yet and it's already afternoon." Worry wrinkled her brow.

A grunt came from beneath their dented county rig, where Hunt lay on his back on a road sign in the middle of their lane, tinkering with the engine. Carolina acted as his assistant, straddling his feet, which—like the wicked witch of the west after Dorothy had landed—were the only part of him that were visible.

"Luckily," he said, "Scruggs will be too distracted by the decimation of his pickup to care about litter."

"Mmm. That's encouraging."

"You want encouragement? Let's see…they can't fire us."

"Bummer." With a quick glance over her shoulder,

Carolina leaned in under the hood and peered through the maze of engine parts to Hunt's face. "You don't think they'll be back, do you?"

"Who? Dumb and Dumber? Nah."

She shivered. "I hope not."

Hunt scratched his nose with his wrist. "They're long gone."

Carolina settled her weight on her sore ankle to test its strength. It was better already. She could run, if she had to, though it didn't really matter. Hunt was probably right. Old Ted and Willie weren't coming back.

The way Hunt had come rumbling up in that apartment house of a John Deere, just as Ted and Willie had spotted her, why the two of them had turned tail without a backward glance and sped off. A satisfied smile tugged at her lips. Her view of Hunt was ever changing. Life had sure as heck been anything but boring lately.

From the Kuenzis—who lived a good two miles down the road—Hunt had borrowed a tractor, a tow chain and a complete set of auto mechanic's tools. Apparently, Wayne Kuenzi had been on Hunt's football team back in high school and they were still great buddies.

Much to Carolina's chagrin, while Hunt was at the Kuenzis' place, he'd put in a call to the Hidden Valley Police Department and reported their "fender-bender" to Selma. Selma had said Scruggs was on a Code 7—which everyone in town knew was a trip to Starbucks—and she didn't know exactly when he'd return and give them approval to call a tow truck.

Fine with Carolina.

She wasn't exactly anxious to get a gander at the look on the officer's face when he saw what she'd done to the new rig. It was pitiful. Once Hunt had dragged the truck back up on the road, they could see that the main damage was to the tailgate and rear bumper. And the entire passenger side.

Everything else was in pretty good shape. Comparatively speaking. Now, if they could only get the engine started. Carolina sighed.

"Hand me that smaller socket, there, will ya? No. The other one. Thanks."

His little grunts and heavy breathing as he worked were comforting to Carolina. He knew what he was doing, that was for sure. Very sexy, a man who knew his way around an engine. Especially a shirtless man with streaks of grease on his cheeks and dirt on his chest. The pants of his jumpsuit were filthy and there was straw in his hair, but Carolina had never been more attracted to a man.

She mopped her face with his damp T-shirt, then bunched it under her nose. Smelled good. Like that spicy deodorant that made her think of sea captains and mulled wine and those bars of Ivory soap they got to carve back in the fourth grade.

And…him.

"If you—" she cleared her throat to rid her voice of the dreamy quality "—get this thing running, could we get back to the shop and avoid calling a tow truck?"

"You mean in time to hide this mess from Scruggs?"

"Yes. Although I doubt we can hide it all summer. Unless," she cast him a rueful grin, then brightened, "we always drive with the good side facing Scruggs."

"Okay. We can do that."

Carolina laughed and pushed his shirt under her ponytail and behind her neck to soak up the moisture there. A high-pitched whine alerted her to a mosquito on her arm and she slapped it into a bloody streak. "Never mind. I can handle Scruggs."

"I have no doubt that you can. But I don't think that's such a good idea."

"Why not?"

"Because you don't know what you're playing with there."

Carolina laughed. "Scruggs? Oh, come on. A little harmless flirtation with Officer Dragnet might get us off the hook sooner."

Hunt was silent for a long moment, then said, "Trust me. The more you flirt with Scruggs, the more he'll hang around. Don't toy with him. He's trouble."

She couldn't believe that. Scruggs? The Pillsbury Lawboy? "You make him sound like a weirdo or something."

"No. But he does have a few issues when it comes to relationships. If you know what's good for you, you'll steer clear. Besides, don't you already have your sights set on McGraw?"

She grimaced. "Not anymore. That's over."

"Well that's encouraging."

Carolina gave her brows a waggle. "Why? You thinking about tossing your hat my way?"

"One puny kiss in the kitchen pantry and she thinks I'm hooked and ready to be reeled into the boat."

Before she stopped to consider the consequences, Carolina tipped the water bottle that perched on the flat surface of the truck's battery and let him have a dribble. In the face. Grinning, she watched him gasp.

Her grin faded as he sputtered and pushed himself out from under the truck. By the look in his eye, Carolina knew that she was in trouble. Before her legs could obey her brain's command to move, Hunt had grabbed one of the two water kegs that were stacked on the cooler by the driver's side door.

She screamed, half in horror, half in glee. Legs finally in gear, she hobbled around the crumpled tailgate, slid down into the ditch, scrambled up the other side and ran pell-mell into the wheat field. All the while, she hollered at the top of her lungs.

The top half of her jumpsuit flapped at her thighs and her sleeves tangled at her ankles. This, coupled with her initial indecision and her sore ankle, had placed her at a disadvantage. Seemed Hunt still had his football wheels, even in the heat. He carried the keg under his arm like a pro with his pigskin, unscrewing the top as he ran. In no time, he'd caught up with her and held it over her head. "A little retribution?"

"Never!" Shrieking, she braced his arms at the elbows with her palms. "Get back, bucko!" Her words were filled with punch-drunk laughter.

"Oh, but I owe you, my little Carolina honey. My little barbecue pork rib—"

She gasped. *"Pork* rib!"

"—and I always pay my bills."

"No! Don't! That's the only drinking water we have!"

The water sloshed wildly over the top of the plastic insulated two-gallon keg.

"No, it's not. Selma was very thoughtful and packed another one of these for us."

Hooting with hilarity and something akin to sunstroke, Carolina wobbled around in the wheat, pushing at his torso and trying to escape the hand that held her wrist in a vise grip.

"Officer Scruggs is going to be really mad if he catches us clowning around and not doing our job."

"He's gonna be mad, but not about our so-called job."

Carolina was giggling like a loon. "Get to work, bucky."

"Not until you've had a shower. You stink."

"I *stink? Me?* I beg your pardon."

"Ah, she's begging again. I have a powerful effect on you, huh, woman?"

The keg tipped, sloshing back and forth in their arms.

"Quit, it, Hunt. I mean it. If you pour water on me, I'll kick you in the ya-yas."

"Now she's jabbering about my ya-yas."

"I am *not,* you big *boob!*"

"What's this about boobs? Don't tell me you have another mammo appointment now."

Carolina's hilarity traversed the scale. "I'm *serious,* get back!"

She attempted to bolt, but it was useless. Hunt was faster and stronger and before she knew it, he had her pinned to the mashed wheat on the ground and with a tilt of the keg, a cascade of heart-stoppingly cold ice water flooded over her head and torso.

She gasped and squealed, shook her head and palmed the water out of her eyes. It felt heavenly, but she'd never tell him that, the big galoot.

On his knees and bent backward, Hunt roared with belly laughter.

"How *dare* you?"

"I dare because while I do all the work, you are dreaming up schemes to flirt with that bozo."

"You do *not* do all the work!"

Hunt slopped another quart of water into her face.

Eyes closed, she coughed and then reached out and swung at him and missed. "Okay," she sputtered. "You do a lot of the work. But I don't know anything about engines, okay!"

Another blast of water hit her in the face and she screamed.

"Or driving?"

"Okay! Or driving! I'll admit *that*."

"Or men."

"Hey! If I'm flirting with that bozo, it's because I'm trying to get on his good side so that he'll let us out of our sentence."

"Oh, so now you are flirting with Scruggs for *my* sake."

"Yes! And you are not *appreciating my sacrifice!*" She pulled up a clump of wheat and hurled it at him. As he held up the keg and took aim, Carolina rose to her knees, and they wrestled over its ownership until they both fell over. The rest of the water spilled over them and the dusty ground, leaving a small mud slick.

Wanting to get away from the ooze, Carolina attempted to stand, but slipped and fell. Mud spattered everywhere. Bits of hay clung to the goo on her clothes.

Hunt took one look at her and hooted with laughter. "You look like Scruggs's back seat."

Lips twitching, she bit back a giggle. She didn't want to give Hunt the satisfaction of finding his remark amusing.

However, when Hunt stood, skated a bit and then took a plunge backward, she could contain herself no longer. She dropped down next to him and there they lay side by side on a prickly bed of wheat and held their bellies as they rolled around and laughed.

And laughed.

"That truck was brand spanking new."

Carolina tried to look indignant. "It still is. It's just…"

"Running a little rough. You can tell Scruggs you were just working out a few kinks."

They howled at that.

"Yeah. I'll tell him it was the truck's fault. We'll sue!"

"I say we sue Scruggs. Clearly, you didn't know how to drive."

"Okay! This whole thing is *his* fault!" Tears of laughter streamed down her cheeks as Carolina flailed her feet in the wheat.

"We are so dead." Hunt groaned.

"Back to jail. Do not pass go."

"Do not collect two hundred dollars."

"Ohh. My stomach hurts," Carolina said, and rolled into a ball on her side.

The sun blazed, drying the mud on their skin. The slightest of breezes ruffled their hair and felt good on their damp clothing. For a long moment after their laughter had tapered off to the occasional chuckle, they lay there, watching each other and smiling.

From beneath the fringe of her lashes, she watched the various emotions pass through his eyes until they became dark and mysterious. Nearly smoldering. Tension radiated between them as they lay, mere inches apart.

Plucking a blade of wheat from the ground, Hunt turned on his side and ran its grain-filled end in a featherlight circle around the perimeter of her face. Motionless, Carolina held her breath and watched his eyes flash over her face and settle on her mouth. Her heart thrummed in her throat as the strand of wheat moved slowly over her jaw, to her chin to her lower lip. It tickled, so she pulled her lip between her teeth and rubbed it with her tongue.

His expression grew more intense as he pushed himself up on an elbow and probed her eyes with his gaze.

There it was again. That same feeling that had shimmered between them back in the pantry. She met his deep, clear-eyed gaze with her own, and a twinge of guilt niggled. Though she was loath to admit it, she owed him a huge apology. He'd been so helpful in so many ways, and she'd been…well, she'd been a brat. Pure and simple. Oh, she liked to give a lot of lip service to being fair and nonjudgmental, but when the chips were down, she was as self-centered as the next spoiled billionaire's niece.

She was suddenly ashamed. Embarrassed at her horrible behavior on the Fourth of July. And in the courthouse. And on the road, today. It wasn't like her to play the shrew.

The worst part of all was, her pride had kept her from owning up to her part in this whole debacle. Her father would disown her. She sighed. And her mother would write up the paperwork.

It was time.

Slowly she reached out, placed a hand on Hunt's shoulder and pushed a little space between them so that she could clearly see his face. "I need to say something to you."

"Uh-oh."

"Shh." His bemused smile was all Carolina needed. Up on her knees, she pushed him on his back and braced one hand on either side of his body. She hovered over him, nose to nose. "I'm sorry," she murmured in a repentant voice. Her hair fell in a wet curtain of ropes around their faces, shading them from the sun.

"For what?"

"I've been a brat."

"Oh. That. Yeah. You have. Really. You have been a real pain in th—"

"Okay." She clapped her hand over his lips. Soft lips, with a hit of rough beard at the edges. Very sexy. "Now that we agree on that, I also want to thank you."

"An apology and a thank-you? Did I die in that wreck? Is this heaven?"

"Be serious."

"Sorry." He arranged his face into a pose of contrition.

"Thank you for saving my butt. Several times."

"You're welcome." His eyes slid to a lazy half-mast. Her heart began to pound. "Several times."

Their gaze held. Moments passed.

Her whisper was barely audible. "You're not as horrible as I thought."

"Neither are you."

"This doesn't mean I like you."

Hunt thrust out his lower lip. "No?"

"No. But, I'm working on it."

"Mmm."

Prodding his nose with hers, her eyes slid closed and she searched for, and finally found his mouth. Oh, so lightly she feathered his lips with her own. "Forgive me?" She breathed his rapid breath, still drifting above him like a butterfly, but refusing to land with any weight. Her arms began to shake with the exertion it took to keep herself at bay.

"Yeah."

"You," she whispered, "do have certain qualities."

"Mmm-hmm. You, too."

Cupping her face in his palms, Hunt looked deep into her eyes, then, seeming to find what he was looking for, pulled her mouth against his in a full-bodied exchange that had Carolina collapsing against his chest, lost in the moment.

Dreamlike moments passed as the sun cast long dappled shadows over their faces and bodies. The wheat whispered its soft music under the light touch of the breeze, and a meadowlark accompanied it with its own lilting melody. It was a phenomenal kiss, far more potent than the one they'd shared in the pantry, and *that* one had left her reeling for the better half of the day. But this was the second kiss. They were a bit more familiar now with each other's ways and felt secure in their explorations.

Like a free fall from a plane, Carolina reveled in the

giddy, dizzying, stupefying feeling of lying in Hunt's arms. Who knew that a muggy afternoon, in the middle of a wheat field, could be so like heaven? She sighed with a mixture of excitement and contentment.

Mmm. This was so much better than fighting.

Hunt rolled them over so that Carolina was on her back and he was leaning over her. His sexy smile had her heart beating crazily, and her arms slid up to loop around his neck. Again he kissed her with a dizzying passion that had her forgetting time. And space. And everything in between.

Until he froze.

Drawing back, she searched his face with her eyes. What was it?

Motionless, he squinted off into the horizon, and then his eyes fell closed in disgust. "Uh-oh. We've got company." He pulled himself to his knees.

"Who?"

"Scruggs approaching. And his stupid lights are flashing." From where he knelt over her, Hunt rocked back on his heels and shaded his eyes against the sun.

Carolina groaned at his reference to the light that looked, for all the world, like a bubble-gum machine perched atop the speeding cruiser. "Is it too late to run away?"

Hunt stood and offered her his hand. "I thought you said you could handle Scruggs."

"Yeah." She levered herself to her feet. Reaching into her pocket, she withdrew a lipstick and, heedless of the mud spattered strategically about her person, applied a dewy coat and then sighed. "I can handle him. But the question is, do I want to?"

Hunt's expression was grim. "No. You don't."

"Hunt, I think a bit of honey will keep this fly from tossing us back in the brig."

The muscles jumped in his jaw. "You know, I thought maybe, just maybe that for an insane moment, you were above using people to suit your purpose."

"I'm not using him. I'm simply being nice. What on earth is wrong with that? Being rude to him certainly isn't going to get us out of here any sooner. Besides, he's not so bad, once you get to know him."

"Whatever." With a sharp shake of his head, Hunt stalked to the truck and waited for Scruggs. He didn't have to wait long.

The shock on Scruggs's face was evident even before he disembarked from the squad car. Without a word he strolled around the truck in a cloud of disbelief.

"I did it."

It was Hunt's turn to stare as Carolina stated the truth without flinching.

"It was all my fault. I…don't know how to drive. Except for Big Daddy's driveway, I've never driven before in my life."

"Never?"

"I was too embarrassed to admit it. It looks a whole lot easier than it is."

Scruggs swallowed, gripped the mangled tailgate for balance and breathed for a moment. "Well, I guess we could say you owe me." He lifted a brow.

"I plan on never driving again, if that helps."

The officer fingered what was left of the broken taillight. "Not exactly what I had in mind, but it's a start."

Carolina had never been so tired in her entire life. She trudged through Big Daddy's kitchen and made it to a bar stool where she sprawled out across the marble island and slurped up the fresh cup of coffee that Cook had prepared for his own break. With a bemused smile, Cook moved away to brew a fresh pot. Head in her hands, Carolina hoped for just enough caffeine buzz to get her through anger management class that night without falling asleep.

What a day.

Her long groan echoed from within her mug.

What a hell of a day.

Although, it had had its moments. For one thing, Scruggs seemed to be more concerned about her well-being than that of the truck. They could use the old truck till the new one was out of the shop, he'd said, then pulled a frosty cold diet soda from his cooler and handed it to her, while completely ignoring Hunt. He'd also brought her a package of biscotti from Starbucks. Nothing for Hunt.

That's because one caught more flies with honey, Carolina mused, then yawned. Maybe now Hunt would see the beauty of her attitude toward the law. She knew Scruggs's type. Hungry for approval. And a little bit of harmless approval never hurt anyone.

"As long as it's not the kind of approval that gives him the wrong idea," Hunt had told her on the drive home.

"He knows he's not my type."

"Just because he's not some blue-blooded snob doesn't mean he's not vulnerable to the attention of one."

Mouth agape, she'd only been able to gasp. That had stung. Bad. And here she thought they'd finally begun a tentative friendship. Guess not. And after she'd humbled herself with an apology to him and Scruggs and everything. Oh, well.

The sound of tentative footsteps at the kitchen door had her glancing up. Georgia. She emitted another groan into her mug. Oh, brother.

She'd forgotten. Brandon. And Georgia. They had some 'splainin' to do. But *now?* She could barely keep her eyes open, let alone spar with her sister.

"Hey," she mumbled, her lips propped on the rim of her mug.

Georgia helped herself to the last cup of coffee and joined Carolina at the island. "Hey."

"So." Lolling cheek to bicep, Carolina eyeballed her sister.

Georgia cleared her throat. "How was work today?"

"Ghastly. How was your date with Brandon?"

"Okay, let's just get one thing straight. It wasn't exactly a date."

"What *exactly* was it then?"

"Well, when Brandon called to 'talk' I thought it would be a good time to set him straight. You know, tell him off on your behalf and all that stuff."

Carolina arched a brow. Interesting. "Go on."

"He really caught me off guard with the horse ride thing, but I went along with it because I figured we'd be on my turf, and it would be easier for me to tell him off."

Carolina nodded.

"But when he got here, he was so nice, bringing me candy and stuff, that I couldn't tell him off right then. Timing is everything, as you know."

"Right." That lesson had come up a few times today, as a matter of fact.

"Anyway, I remembered that you said Brandon was really a pretty nice guy, just confused, and I thought maybe instead of telling him off, it might be better to let him down gently, especially if there was a chance that he might get back together with you, because then he would end up being my *brother*-in-law, for heaven's sake and I hardly wanted hurt feeling's between us, if I could help it."

With a noncommittal shrug, Carolina took a sip of her coffee. Made sense.

"Anyway," Georgia continued, "he had packed a picnic, and told me that he was so sorry about the way that things turned out between him and you and that he really needed to talk. I thought he wanted to talk about you, so I agreed."

Carolina gave her sister a bleary once-over. "But he really wanted to talk about a possible future with you."

A salsa-red blush stained Georgia's cheeks. "Uh-huh."

It was surprising how dispassionate she felt about the whole thing. Perhaps she needed time to digest everything that had happened to her in the past week. Gulping down the dregs in her cup, Carolina pushed herself to her feet and saluted her sister. "We'll continue this when I'm not dead on my feet, 'kay?"

"He didn't try to kiss me or anything, if that makes you feel better."

It was Carolina's turn to feel the stab of guilt. "Thanks." She sighed and smiled at Georgia as she moved out of the room. "I have to go get ready for my anger management class tonight."

Georgia's eyes grew round. "Oh. Okay. Good luck."

"Don't look at me that way."

"What way?"

"That scared-rabbit way. Like I have a problem with anger." She waved and moved up the stairs and into the hall where she slogged to her suite. She shut the door behind her and leaned against its smooth surface and pondered her predicament. It was all so very conflicting. Her. Brandon. Georgia. Hunt. Scruggs. Relationships weren't the superficial fun they used to be a mere week ago.

No. She pushed off the door and headed up to her shower.

Nothing was the same anymore.

* * *

As angry as she was about the way he had goaded her about her budding friendship with Scruggs, Carolina couldn't help but feel a surge of renegade joy at the sight of Hunt waiting for her in the kitchen that evening. He also was freshly showered and dressed in clean clothes that set off his physique to perfection. Even as her heart knocked about beneath her ribs, Carolina steeled herself against his potent allure. He still had her shoved into an unfair stereotype.

He didn't seem to get the fact that she was a Brubaker. Brubakers had scruples. Just because they were rich and—she shoved her fingers into her scalp and gave her hair a practiced fluffing—above-average in looks, didn't make them elitist or superior. Lips pursed, she swallowed her smile of greeting and marched past.

Since they were running late, they grabbed the hamper of sandwiches and coffee Cook had prepared for them and headed to Hunt's rig.

After depositing the hamper in the back seat of his SUV, he held open the passenger door for her and motioned for her to take her seat. "I'll drive, if you don't have any objection."

She shrugged and groped for a stinging retort, but his hand at her back rendered her speechless.

There was a broad grin at his lips as he swung around to his side and climbed in behind the wheel.

Covertly, Carolina watched Hunt start his engine and studied the way he used the clutch as he maneuvered through the gears. Hmm. Fascinating. Now she wished she hadn't spent so much time flirting with Miles Billingsly in the back seat of the car during driver's ed. Accelerator depressed to go, accelerator up and clutch down to shift, clutch up, then accelerator depressed again. Looked simple enough.

When he did it.

Leaning slightly forward to better study this seemingly smooth orchestration, she mouthed the words as Hunt rounded the corner from the driveway and onto the highway. "Gas, gas up, clutch down, shift, clutch up, gas down." She frowned. The timing was so complex. And just how, exactly, did he know when to shift?

As if he could read her mind, Hunt said, "For the first twenty miles an hour, it's best in first gear. After twenty, you want to move to second gear. At thirty, third. At forty, forth. If you have a five speed, you shift to fifth gear, or overdrive, at fifty and leave it there until you need to slow down."

So interested was she that Carolina forgot the chip on her shoulder. "How do you slow down?"

"To save wear and tear on your brake pads, it's best to start shifting down well before you have to stop. That'll slow ya down, then you can push in the clutch and brake at your stop, without killing the engine."

"So that's the secret." She tossed her head. "I could do that. Not that I want to."

"Anyone can drive a stick." Hunt agreed with a genial nod. "Just takes practice. In fact, you should drive."

"Who? Me? No thanks, I'm trying to cut down."

Hunt snorted. "I thought you were one to get back up on the horse."

"Forget it. I have Basil. I have public transportation. That's all I need. I meant it when I said I was never going to drive again."

"Oh, come on." His lip curled. "Hidden Valley has no public transportation, unless you count our carriage company. You are living in a new millennium. You need to learn to be independent."

"I am independent."

"Prove it. Get back on the damned horse." Hunt

jerked the wheel, and before she knew what was happening, he'd turned down a deserted road, pulled to the shoulder and killed the engine. He beckoned her to climb up and over his lap and into the driver's seat. "Come on. Let's get at it."

"Forget it."

"We're not going anywhere until you climb up here and give it a go." Grin lascivious, he patted his lap.

Carolina giggled. "Never. I told you. I'm never driving again. Period."

"Good evening. Mr. And Mrs….?"

"Crenshaw," Hunt supplied without bothering to correct the assumption that they were a married couple.

"Crenshaw. Yes. You're late. Please sign the roster and then take a seat."

The anger management instructor—whose name tag read: Hello! My Name Is Mrs. Cullpepper—offered them a clipboard and a tight smile as Carolina and Hunt entered room 112 at East Central Dallas Community College. Hunt scrawled The Crenshaws into the allotted space and handed the roster back to Mrs. Cullpepper.

As they moved away, Carolina elbowed him and bristled. "I'm perfectly capable of writing my own name."

"Mm-kay." Hunt took a moment to survey the nearly empty room and select their seats. "Go write it."

"Not *now*. Now she already thinks we're 'the Crenshaws.'"

"So? It's not like we plan on playing pinochle with her and Mr. Cullpepper. Who cares who we are? I'm not going to quibble with the anger teacher."

He had a point.

The musty-smelling classroom was the typical institutional setup, the walls a cool toothpaste green, probably meant to soothe, the floor was a gravel-pattern linoleum, and the desks, simple wooden chairs with one extra-wide armrest. The clock above the chalkboard showed a quarter past the hour.

"Good evening. You're late. Please sign the roster and then take a seat," Mrs. Cullpepper said to the next people entering the room.

"Yeah, well we had a flat tire, okay? Geez."

"Manny, the nice lady was just sayin'—"

"I know what she was *sayin'*, Loretta."

With a glance at Hunt, Carolina rubbed her jaw where his five-o'clock shadow had given her a bit of whisker burn during their nondriving-driving lesson. Hunt nodded at a pair of seats near the back. "C'mon."

Wordlessly Carolina followed him. They settled in together near the back of the room. Hands wringing, nerves jangling, Carolina took a moment to give her arriving classmates a covert look-see.

To the woman settling behind her, she shot a tentative smile.

"Take a picture, it lasts longer," the woman snapped.

"I…well…yes. Thank you." Nonplussed, Carolina twisted back around in her seat and glanced at Hunt, who was busy watching two clearly inebriated men stagger to the front seats while holding a rather boisterous conversation about this needless waste of their personal time, and how it always cut into happy hour down at Slick Chick's.

As the teacher ground the importance of promptness into the blackboard with a stubby piece of chalk, stragglers of all walks of life continued to shuffle in and find seats.

"Good evening. You're late. Please sign the roster and then take a seat." Chalk dust flew.

An old man moved to an empty desk in the back row

and promptly fell into a sound sleep. A group of teenage boys pushed and shoved each other into a neighboring group of seats. The Illustrated Man's identical twin dropped into the chair in front of Carolina, and her jaw fell slack in awe. It was most amazing. Every available inch of flesh depicted flaming images of death. A skull complete with—was that a tongue?—leered at her from the back of his neck until he turned in his chair to greet her.

"Hi." Unabashed, his flashing eyes roved her form from head to toe.

"Hello." Carolina swallowed. Gracious. His face brimmed with more studs than a snow tire and his lipstick was a most delicate shade of black.

"Whatcha in for?"

"Uh, me?" She pointed to her chest. "Here?"

"She's with me," Hunt said and, reaching across the aisle, took Carolina's hand in his own. For once she didn't argue at his arrogant, overprotective tone.

"You two duke it out? Yeah. I hear that. My old lady got a restraining order for my birthday." Guffaws accompanied the scraping of his chair as he turned to check out the other women in the room.

"That's…nice." Carolina motioned for Hunt to bend close and whispered, "Do we really look like these people?"

He glanced around. "You do."

His sense of humor relaxed her some. He smelled good. Compelling. Familiar. The recesses of her brain had registered his scent as alluring and sent a surge of adrenaline coursing through her body every time she got this near.

"Class? May I have your attention please?" The instructor presented a toothy smile as she began to introduce the course, although, much to her dismay, no one paid much heed. "Please take one copy of these materials and pass them back—"

"I should have worn more makeup," Hunt mouthed with a grin.

"—to study on your own time."

"Hilarious. You know," Carolina clutched his sleeve and tugged his ear to her lips, "I think I saw a picture of him on a poster, back when we were in jail."

"…section titled 'The Origins of the Anger Response'…"

"Really?" Hunt leaned in till their foreheads touched.

Carolina nodded and scooted her chair-desk combo into the aisle up next to his chair. The Tattooed Man passed back a stack of literature. "Thank you very, very much." With a wide, ingratiating—and fear-filled smile—she took one for herself and one for Hunt and passed the rest to the grump behind her. "Yes. I'm sure of it. While you were having your mug shot taken, I had time to look them all over."

Irritation flashed in the instructor's eyes. "…study of the crucial 'trigger event,' the moment at which your anger flares…"

"What was he wanted for?"

She frowned. "Arson, I think."

"Criminy. What the hell are we doing here?"

Lips bunched into a wad of sarcasm, Carolina said, "We're a menace to society, remember?"

"I guess…"

One of the teens raised his hand.

"Yes, uh—" the instructor scanned her clipboard "—Reggie?"

"Yo. I'm down wit what you sayin'. One o' my posse had a trigger event. 'Most blowed his bu—"

"Thank you, Mr. er…Reggie, but the trigger event I refer to is an emotional trigger not the one on your…uh, gun." Jaw grim, veins in her neck bulging, the instructor held up a finger. "Weapons, by the way, are not allowed in class."

Several students exchanged glances. One man left.

Eyes wide, Carolina strained toward Hunt and whispered, "Are we safe here?"

"Probably more now than we were a second ago."

"These people give me the willies. I want to go home."

"We can't just 'go home.'"

"Why not? That one guy just did."

"Because Judge Scruggs says we have to tough it out. Stop being such a pantywaist."

"Judge Scruggs didn't say we had to hang around with these…these felons!" she hissed.

"Mr. and Mrs. Crenshaw?" Nostrils flaring, the instructor clapped her hands. The class all joined her and turned to stare at Hunt and Carolina. Heads together, they had no idea they'd become the center of attention. Even the sleeping man stopped snoring.

"You can't make me stay."

Mrs. Cullpepper frowned. "Mrs. Crenshaw, please—"

"You're not leaving without me."

"You can't tell me what to do!"

"Mr. and Mrs. Crenshaw!" The instructor slammed her text on her desk. "I'm going to have to ask you to please focus on the material!"

The Tattooed Man finally turned around and pounded on Carolina's desk. "Hey! You! Woman! Shut the hell up!"

Hunt's chair clattered to the floor as he leaped to his feet. His voice was dangerously low. "Talk to her like that again, scum bucket, and I'll feed you a fist sandwich."

And that was all it took for the melee to commence.

Chapter Eight

"Hunter Crenshaw, I can't believe *you,* of all the emotionally controlled people I've ever known, got thrown out of anger management class. That's a riot."

Hunt's aunt Rita shook her head as she reached into the frozen foods section and tossed her nephew a bag of frozen peas for the bruise on his jaw. Still youthful and cute as a bug's ear in her late forties, Rita liked to get her grocery shopping done in the middle of the night. Couldn't abide lines. So she usually commandeered someone from the family to come with her on her midnight forays.

Since he'd made the mistake of dropping by her house after class, Hunt was elected. Too bad he was so beat. Literally and figuratively. As usual, all thanks to Carolina Brubaker.

Piped-in elevator music filled the empty aisles of the 25-Hour CartMart with some semblance of humanity, but precious little. Man, it was like a morgue in here. All he wanted was his bed. Holding the peas to his jaw, he yawned, and slogged after his aunt who wielded her cart like a Sherman tank through the produce section.

He knew she'd forced him to come for a reason. As usual, she wanted to talk. To probe. To be there for him, clucking, fussing and trying to get him to act like one of the brood as she had since the day his mother had died.

And Lord knew, he'd tried. But in the early years raw grief had held him emotionally aloof from the mother/son connection he yearned for, until after he'd moved out of the house and begun to mature. And heal. So now he was getting the mothering he'd missed out on as a kid. God help him.

"Grab a bag of spuds, there, will ya, buddybuns?" Rita whipped her cart up the fruit aisle and began to thump melons. "Yesh. This one's nearly as bruised as you are." She laughed over her shoulder. "Really, I thought we'd brought you up better than this." She pointed at the oozing, broken melon.

"Ha." Hunt rolled his eyes and hefted a ten-pound bag of potatoes into the cart. "Don't go and get all holier-than-thou with me. I heard about you and Becky cat fighting over Uncle Mike.

Rita's rich laughter was culture in audio form. "He tell you about that?" She thrust a cantaloupe into his chest.

"Yep. Seems you were a bit of a snoot."

"Yes, but I mellowed nicely. Go on now." She propelled her cart over to the broccoli section and began to weed through the crowns and called across the bin. "Tell me about all this community service stuff you have to perform."

Hunt winced. Luckily there were only one or two other lunatics out grocery shopping at this time of night and they were in another section.

"It seems a little excessive, don't you think?"

"What I think doesn't seem to matter anymore. Anyway, to make a long, long, very idiotic story a short idiotic story, suffice it to say that I won't be around much this summer to help you guys with the carriage business."

"That's okay. Judah and Evan are filling in nicely."

"Yeah, well, that's not really fair to them."

"Sure it is." Aunt Rita bagged a pile of broccoli, tossed it to him and moved to thoughtfully fondle the tomatoes. By her pensive body posture, Hunt could tell she was cranking up for one of her motherly spiels. Frozen peas to throbbing jaw, he leaned back against the rutabagas and settled in for the long haul.

"Honey—" Aunt Rita eyed him from between sale signs "—I think this break from ranching will do you good. Get you out of the stables and into the real world for a moment."

"I'm in the real world." Where did she think he spent his days? Roping rainbows?

"I know, I know. But your uncle Mike and I were so inexperienced when you boys came to live with us that we hardly knew what to do with our grief, let alone yours." The piped-in elevator music was now a rousing polka, an odd contrast to her solemn words. "Hunt, you were always such a serious young boy. In a way I feel responsible for that. When your mother passed on, you took it so hard and worried so much about your brothers' grades and behaviors and such and…well, you were still just a kid yourself."

Hunt moved down the aisle to the cart and tossed in the frozen peas. Rita cradled a tomato between her hands and rubbed its shiny skin with her thumbs.

"You grew up far faster than any little boy should have. I think you never learned to simply have fun for the sake of having fun." She dropped the tomato in a bag and selected several more, then put them atop the pile in her cart. "I think that this Carolina Brubaker might just be a gift from heaven. Teach you how to play."

Hunt pointed to the bruise on his jaw. "Big fun."

"Yes, but for once at least you weren't cow punching."

"You're funny as a rubber crutch tonight."

She reached up and cradled his bruise with a mother's loving hand. With a grin at the overhead speaker she said, "Dance with me, lumpy."

In spite of his pain and the hour and the fact that he'd been tossed out of class, Hunt pulled her into his arms and waltzed her around a pyramid of eggplants.

"You have feelings for her, you know," Rita said.

"Yeah."

"Big stuff, these feelings."

"Don't rub it in."

"What are you going to do about them?"

Hunt paused and gave her a twirl. "Probably marry her and end up miserable like Uncle Mike."

Rita's laughter rang throughout the store.

"Then, that very night, we got thrown out of anger management class."

A week later Carolina's older sister Ginny paused and fingered the plush ear of a teddy bear at the end of a toy isle in Baby World as she listened to Carolina fill her in on the travails of her community services. Pulling the bear to her chest, she stroked its fur and smiled. "I hear through the university school of psychology grapevine that they let you back into anger management class."

Carolina brandished a Barbie. "Yes, but I had to go *beg* them."

"Good for you. And give Mrs. Cullpepper a chance. She's a bit high-strung, but she's good at what she does."

They'd been strolling up and down the aisles of Baby World that evening for nearly an hour, taking notes and gathering ideas for the tiny nursery that they were preparing for the baby's arrival next spring.

"She is? If you say so. At any rate, I did my homework assignment last night. It was a little test."

"Good."

"I was sorta surprised at how impulsive I am, which, I can see now, has been at the root of a lot of my problems in life." Absently she picked up a Ken doll and wrapped his arms around Barbie, studied their pose, then set them back on the shelf.

Ginny wound their arms together as they strolled. "Carolina, my dear, I do believe you are becoming a lovely young woman."

Carolina blushed at the praise from her exceedingly mature older sibling and reveled at having Ginny all to herself. Times like this were so rare. Now that Ginny lived here in Hidden Valley, and she would be going back to Dallas in the fall, who knew when they'd find the time to simply have a private conversation in person again?

She tilted her head against Ginny's. "Anyway, since then, Hunt and I have done four more hideous days of community service."

Ginny smiled. "And you're still alive to tell the tale?"

"Barely. On Tuesday we answered phones at the senior center. Hunt was the star attraction there, and by lunchtime he'd been proposed to by Ardith Dunnsbury and Edna Centilli. I encouraged him to go for Edna, as she makes a mean cheesecake. I, on the other hand, was courted by Officer Scruggs, who dropped by to check on me and Hunt—"

"Eustace Scruggs…Jr.?" Ginny stopped and tested the fullness of a beautiful bumper pad tied to a hand-carved crib.

"Yeah. You know him?"

Ginny suddenly had that Hippocratic oath look on her face. The one that said she knew a whole boatload more than she could say. "I know of him, yeah."

Curiosity had Carolina bent at the knees and squinting up at her sister. "What?"

"Can't say."

Cheeks puffed, Carolina exhaled. Of course not. "Whatever. Anyway, I think he has a teeny crush on me—"

"Uh-oh."

"What, 'uh-oh?'"

"Nothing."

"Nothing?"

"Nothing serious, anyway. What do you think of this?" Ginny held up a gaudy wall hanging. "Says here that it promotes brilliance. That'd be good."

"Hate it. Promotes nausea."

"Oh, come on. You don't think it's even a little bit cute?"

"No."

"You are so weird. Okay. Continue. You were telling me about the senior center," Ginny prompted.

"Right. Let's see. On Wednesday, we had to help out at Kenny Wilkins's auto body shop, sweeping up and manning the phones while he pounded the dents out of our truck. That was one boring day, I'll tell you. Until Scruggs stopped by with a meatball hoagie for me."

"He always brings you guys lunch?"

"No. Just me."

Ginny frowned and opened her mouth as if to speak, but didn't.

Carolina shrugged. "Then yesterday, we had to stuff envelopes for the Bender Shoe Emporium's Back-to-School Buy One/Get One Free Shoe Sale—"

"Buy one shoe?"

"Yeah, goofy, huh? Anyway, Scruggs stopped by to check on us and brought me the cutest little potted cactus with little eyes glued on and a tiny policeman outfit—"

"Carolina—"

"Hmm? Oh, hang on a sec. Look at *this*. Is this the cutest little outfit you've ever seen? I *have* to get this for your baby. Oh, and I have to tell you what we did today. Baby-sat. For Frank and Judy Shirley. Talk about complete and total *brats*. The boys spent the entire day playing wrestle-mania with Hunt, which basically meant jumping off the furniture and landing on him while he shouted at them to knock it off. The girls got into their mother's makeup and I spent the day cleaning nail polish off the furniture and walls. Did you know nail polish remover bubbles the paint on molding?"

"Interesting. You seem to be getting on better with Hunt these days."

Carolina felt her cheeks grow warm. "We have our moments."

Hunt stood at home plate in the middle of the community softball diamond that had been reinstalled at the fairgrounds the day after the rodeo left town. Bat clutched tightly, he shifted from foot to foot. "You gonna pitch?"

"Hey, batta, batta, hey batta!" Carolina shouted. "Swing. Wadda ya want? Eggs in your beer?"

With a snort, Hunt put the bat's nose on the plate and leaned. "You have to pitch if I'm going to swing, you dweeb."

Carolina giggled. "Oh, yeah." Winding up the way

she'd seen the pros do on TV, she pitched a crumpled pop can. It waffled wildly to the left, but Hunt smashed at it anyway and sent it sailing out toward first base.

"And the crowd goes wild," Carolina screamed and ran after the can.

When she'd reached the pitcher's mound again, Hunt said, "This time, try something else. Something heavier."

"Mm-kay." Carolina rummaged through the bag of trash they'd gathered from the stands earlier that morning and came up with a nearly full plastic bottle of pop. "Ready, batta? Hey, batta?"

"Just pitch." Though he was yelling, it was clear that he found this game highly amusing. "Soft-Trash" was what they called the sport they'd invented. A variation on softball, but much messier. And more fun.

In fact, Carolina had to admit this was the most fun she'd had in ages. Never in all her born days would she have envisioned herself picking up garbage, let alone playing with it. Her hands were filthy, her nail beds abysmal, her jumpsuit a mess, but she'd never been so happy and carefree in her whole life. And after four grueling years in college, she really needed the change.

"Stand back, buddy-boy."

"Put your money where you mouth is."

"Put your mouth where my mouth is."

Hunt dropped the bat and stalked toward the pitcher's mound.

"No!" Carolina shrieked and took off running. "I was just kidding."

But they both knew she wasn't.

It was minimally cooler in the shade of the bleachers, where they'd been taking their lunch all week long.

The fairgrounds nearly gleamed they were so clean. Earlier that morning Carolina had seen a guy toss a cigarette butt into the area she'd just pressure washed and took a moment to deliver a duel lecture on the subjects of littering and the tax payers' dollar. The poor man had picked up his butt and several others lying nearby before she'd finished.

It was always such a relief when lunch hour arrived. Carolina reached into the cooler and handed Hunt his sandwich.

"What did you do over the weekend?" he asked around a mouthful of pastrami on rye.

"Went baby shopping with Ginny." Warily Carolina glanced up at the pigeons that roosted in the rafters overhead. Though sitting in the bleachers was hardly lunch at the Ritz, it felt so wonderful to get off her feet and out of the blistering sun. She propped her feet on the bench below and made a mental note to bring cushions for them to sit on tomorrow. And an umbrella for the pigeons. Just in case.

"Baby shopping? She pregnant?"

"Oops!" Carolina closed her eyes and called herself every kind of big-mouthed fool. "I wasn't supposed to spill the beans. But yes, Ginny's pregnant and only family knows."

"Well then you're okay."

Carolina studied his face. He didn't seem to notice the import of his words. Probably because it was true. He was part of the family.

Holding his sandwich up in salute, Hunt swallowed, then grinned. "A little niece or nephew. That's great."

"Yeah. I'm so happy for them both. They really wanted to have a baby right away."

"I want a lot of kids, too."

"You do?"

"Yeah. I came from a family of three boys, but we lived with my three cousins, so there were really six of us. It was nice."

"Big families are nice." Carolina dug a bottle of iced tea from the chest and held it to her neck. A thrill of gooseflesh crawled down her spine as she sensed Hunt following the motion with his eyes. "You grow up around here?"

"Yup."

"Your folks still live here?"

"No. My folks—" he took a deep breath and angled his head so that he could look her in the eye "—are both dead."

"Oh." Carolina swallowed. "I'm really sorry. I didn't know about your parents. I...should have."

"It's okay. It was a long time ago."

"Who raised you?"

"My dad's brother, Uncle Mike and his wife Rita. My dad was killed in the Vietnam War, and my mom died of cancer when my brothers and I were still pretty young." He turned back to his sandwich.

Why didn't she know that already? How awful for him. She didn't know how she'd have survived without her parents. But she supposed living with Big Daddy and Miss Clarise would have made all the difference. "Wow. So that's why you lived with your cousins. You have two brothers?"

"Yeah. Judah and Evan."

"And your cousins?"

"Two girls and one boy. All in college now. We all went to college."

"Really?"

"Yup. Even me. So, tell me about *your* family. I

know all about Big Daddy's immediate family, but the rest of you come and go and I can't keep up."

Chewing and nodding, Carolina held up four fingers. "Four sisters. Four brothers. Two parents. My father is Big Daddy's younger brother."

"You come from a family of nine kids? Holy cow."

Carolina laughed. "When we all get together with Big Daddy's kids, there are eighteen. And then there are our cousins from Big Daddy's other siblings. It can get very confusing. But I love the chaos. What did you study in college?"

"Business. You?"

"Interior design."

"You gonna be a decorator?"

"I hope so. Although, sometimes I envy Ginny. She lives the simple life now. Part-time career at the university, in love with her man, a baby on the way, which—" she stopped and slugged him in the arm "—you know *nothing* about."

"Right."

"Yoo hoo! Hello, kids! Great, you found the place."

The next day, flanked on each side by what appeared to be hell's gatekeepers, Mrs. William T. Abernathy flung open her screen door and beckoned Hunt and Carolina to join her on her porch. "I'm so glad you're here! I'm running a tad late. Don't be shy. Come meet the puppies."

Fangs bared, ears flat, fur at attention, two horselike hounds crouched beside Mrs. Abernathy and growled. Clasping Carolina's hand and pushing her behind him, Hunt took a giant step back as the dogs' snarls developed into a barrage of vicious canine thunder.

"Don't look them in the eye," he whispered to Carolina. "That ticks off dogs like these."

Carolina nodded, too paralyzed with fear to respond verbally. His heart went out to her. The blood had drained from her face and, fingers fluttering, she reached for his sleeve. Grabbing hold, she tugged him tightly to her side and whimpered.

"What are they?"

"According to Scruggs, they are today's assignment."

"He never mentioned anything about buffalo."

A fierce surge of protection welled up within Hunt, and he knew right then that he'd die for her. If he had to. Strands of saliva dripped from the dogs' jaws. Hopefully, it wouldn't come to that.

"Muffin! Cupcake! Hush!" Mrs. Abernathy clucked and tsked at her dogs as she fastened on a pair of gold earrings. With a frazzled sigh, she turned her attention to Hunt and Carolina. "I'm so glad you're early. I have a bridge tournament and I'm running behind. The girls get so mad at me when I'm late, good grief, you'd think we were headed to a U.N. meeting to discuss nuclear disarmament, the way they razz me. But I can't help it. If I leave Cupcake and Muffin alone in the house for any length of time, well, I might as well just leave the doors open and let the vandals in, for there would surely be less damage."

"Hunt…" Carolina snuggled even closer.

He nodded and cleared his voice. "Uh, Mrs. Abernathy, er…Cupcake there, and uh, Cookie—"

"Muffin."

"Whatever." His goodnatured chuckle rang hollow even in his own ears. "For baked goods, they don't seem too sweet on us."

Laughter grabbed Mrs. Abernathy by the shoulders and pitched her about. "Aren't you a stitch? Don't worry. They'll love you. Okay. Here are their leashes."

Having no choice but to trust Mrs. Abernathy, Hunt

stepped forward and held out his hand. Carolina shuffled after him, never releasing his arm.

"Put them in your pocket. You don't show them these just yet," Mrs. Abernathy advised. "They tend to get a little excited about walking. And—" she produced a Ziploc bag loaded with what looked like fist-size chunks of beef "—here are their treats. Don't show them their treats just yet, as they are a little greedy. Always remember, dogs are pack animals. You are 'alpha dog.'"

"Alpha…dog," Carolina repeated, and glanced at Hunt who could only shrug.

"Yes, remember that, and you'll be fine. Okay. In this little bottle are their medicine tablets. They have to take them at noon, sharp, right after their treats. Vet's orders. Just open their mouths and pop them in—"

Carolina pressed her face into Hunt's shoulder and murmured, "She's kidding, right?"

He exhaled. "Nope."

"Don't let it frighten you if they seem to have a bit of a 'reaction' to the medicine, that's normal—"

Before they could inquire as to the reaction, Mrs. Abernathy's purse began to play a little tune. After much rummaging, she located her phone and yanked off an earring. "Yes, Gladys. I'm on my way. Yes. I am. Cookie exchange day. Yes. I remembered. If you will let me get off the phone, I'll be there in a few minutes. Oh? No, I don't know where she lives. Let me get a pen."

Nattering as she went, Mrs. Abernathy disappeared into the house. The dogs didn't move a muscle.

Hunt, Carolina and the dogs eyed each other with suspicion.

"Hunt," Carolina whispered from between tremulous lips, "I'm really, really, really, really, really scared."

"Yeah. Me, too."

Carolina smashed her body flat against his side, and for a moment Hunt forgot his fears. She was cute when she was terrified. And soft in all the right places.

"You're not supposed to be really, really, really, really, really scared."

"Okay. If it makes you feel any better, I'm only really, really scared."

Carolina's giggle held an edge of hysteria. "Oh, yeah. Lots better." She forced her head under his arm and, looping it around her shoulders, gripped his hand in hers and peered at the dogs. "Do you think they could eat us?"

"Nah. Not all of us. Just the fleshy parts."

"You are not comforting me."

"Sorry." He rubbed her arm.

"Do you think we should run away?"

"Yeah."

"Now?"

"Why not? But don't run. Never run away from a strange dog. That's when they like to chase you."

"Okay, Gladys, bye-bye now." Mrs. Abernathy hung up, grabbed her basket of fancy cookies and rushed across the porch and past them to her car, before they could bolt.

"Damn. Too late."

The dogs loped after her, seeming to believe that they were included in the bridge tournament.

"I can't thank you two enough for taking my babies for their walk this afternoon." Mrs. Abernathy opened her back door and tossed in her purse and the basket. "Cupcake! No, get out! Get off the cookies, Muffin! Get out of the car this instant!"

Thoroughly cowed, the two dogs slunk out of the car and crouched at her feet.

"All right. Where was I? Oh, yes. Muffin likes to

walk up to the old abandoned Blandish place and 'explore' and Cupcake likes to dig in the woods behind the house. Sometimes she will find a bone, and sometimes, she will do her business. Be sure to bring a plastic bag with you—" she winked "—just in case. Tootles." Mrs. Abernathy jumped into her car, threw it into reverse, bumped over the curb and was off.

Chapter Nine

The canines seemed to have a change of heart about their walkers once Hunt tossed them the bag of treats. Like piranhas, they wolfed down the beef chunks and sniffed around for more. When Hunt showed them their leashes, they lunged at him, paws to shoulders and brayed their impatience in his ears. Carolina shook her head. A lesser man would have been bowled over.

A man like Brandon, for instance.

As she watched Hunt corral the dogs and get them leashed, Carolina thought about her future. When she'd pictured herself married, it had always been to a man like Brandon, but now? The fact she'd ever even been attracted to Brandon in the first place was a mystery. Yes, he was a gentleman and they shared a mutual social circle and had similar advantages as children, but beyond that? Carolina tried to envision a life with him, but the picture was bleak. Depressing. Boring. Certainly there was none of the passion she shared with…she turned and focused on Hunt as a startling realization dawned.

She'd gone and fallen in love with Hunt. Without her consent, her traitorous heart had taken the plunge. Her mouth fell open and the traitor skipped several key beats.

The very man she loathed more than any other man she'd ever had the misfortune to meet was also the very man who made her feel alive. Connected. Protected. Loved.

Slowly the realization dawned that she needed someone like Hunt. The way Ginny needed a man like Colt.

"Hey, dopey, are you just gonna stand there like a bump on a log, or are you going to help?" Hunt demanded, startling her out of woolgathering.

Well, at least he wasn't bowled over by her looks and somewhat formidable financial portfolio. She had to admire him for that. She grinned.

"Where are they going?" she shouted, taking off after him.

"Heck if I know," he called over his shoulder. "C'mon! Run!"

Winded and hot, Carolina trotted after Hunt and the dogs to the top of the hill where the old Blandish place stood at the edge of a huge, empty lot. They'd finally captured the leashes, and at least felt as if they had a modicum of control. Although Carolina had to admit the dogs were ill mannered and embarrassing all the way up the steep incline. They dug up flowerbeds on private property, vandalized fire hydrants, terrorized squirrels and cats and generally ran amok in ways that made Cujo look like a lap dog. And though they seemed to have no respect for any command given by their walkers—her shoulder socket would never be the same—

Carolina wasn't going to quibble. She and Hunt were alive.

And they were together.

The very thought made her happy. And at the same time, apprehensive. She loved him, but how did he feel? It was clear there was a considerable amount of passion behind his kisses. But was it a loving passion? Or simply a controlling passion. She exhaled and pushed her hair out of her face. They did seem to spend a great deal of their time in a power struggle.

Which, personally, she enjoyed. Did he?

When they arrived in the ancient Blandish estate's overgrown gardens they—with an exchange of beleaguered glances—unclipped the leashes and let the dogs have the run of the place.

The sun was now high in the sky and the heat, as usual, relentless. Dry, brown grass crunched under their feet, and grasshoppers leaped before them as they huffed toward the rotten porch for some respite. Abandoned for over a quarter century now, the old Blandish mansion was boarded up, condemned and in regrettable shape. No Trespassing signs were posted everywhere, but neither Cupcake nor Muffin paid them any heed.

With a tired groan, Carolina dropped down next to Hunt on the top step and reveled in the cool shade. Off in the distance they could hear the dogs in hot pursuit of some poor animal, but up here in the seclusion of the Blandish property, it didn't really matter. A small plane's engine rumbled overhead and other than the occasional car down on the main road, it was silent. Peaceful.

Several languid minutes passed before Hunt broke the stillness.

"I used to come up here all the time when I was a kid."

"You did?"

"Mmm-hmm. My cousins and my brothers would always dare each other to come up here at night with a sleeping bag and spend the night inside the house. Alone."

Trying to envision Hunt as a young boy, Carolina leaned back on her elbows and smiled dreamily into the past. "Why?"

"Something to do, I guess. This place was supposed to be haunted."

"That's spooky."

"That's what all the kids used to say. Probably still do."

"So, who's the ghost?"

"Old Man Blandish. The guy who built the house. Legend has it that he built it for his sweetheart, but she up and married someone else, so he lived here by himself and got all bitter and mean. Finally died here, all alone. Nobody missed him, so he'd been dead for a long time before anyone ever found him."

"How sad. And disgusting."

"Mmm." Hunt laughed.

The planet slowed some in its rotation.

And Carolina fell more deeply in love.

"So did you?" Carolina rolled onto one hip and regarded Hunt's handsome profile. She could sit just like this all day, her eyes sweeping slowly over him, drinking in the cut of his biceps, the swell of his chest, the chiseled fullness of his lips. She longed to reach out and touch him again, just because.

"Did I what?" Hunt angled his chin and looked at her from beneath heavy lids.

Her stomach turned over. "Did you ever spend the night here, when you were a little boy?"

"Are you kidding?" A chuckle rumbled deep in his chest. "This place is haunted."

* * *

After a lazy hour spent lounging in the shade and learning about some of the pranks pulled in the Blandish place, it was finally time to round up the dogs and get them home. When Hunt whistled, they both came bounding up, tongues lolling, tails wagging, as if they'd forgotten Mrs. Abernathy was alive, let alone being their "alpha dog."

"Hey, weren't we supposed to give the dogs some kind of pills at noon?"

"Yeah." Hunt glanced at his watch and pulled a small, orange bottle from his pocket. "She says we're supposed to just pop them in their mouths."

"I don't know. They seem so happy with us now. I'd hate for that to change. And weren't we supposed to give it to them after they've had their 'treats' or they'll have some kind of reaction?"

"Too late now." Hunt shook two pills into his palm. "Besides, the vet said promptly at noon, and we're already late. Here, Muffy. Here Cookie."

"Cupcake."

"Whatever." He held out the pills and the dogs snarfed them down like ambrosia. "Okay. Let's go."

They'd just reached the edge of town when Cupcake stopped walking, hunched over and began to heave. He heaved and foamed and growled and whimpered and heaved some more. Then, he dropped to his side, rolled on someone's front lawn and ground his paws into his eyes. Then he stood and chased his tail for a while before starting the heaving routine again.

Carolina and Hunt were helpless to do anything but stand by and gape. First at Cupcake, then at each other, then back at the spinning Cupcake again. It wasn't long before Muffin joined Cupcake for some tandem groaning and foaming and rolling and heaving. And spinning.

"Could this be the normal 'reaction' to the medication that Mrs. Abernathy was trying to tell us about?"

Shoulders bunched, Hunt shook his head. "Normal? For who? Never seen anything like it in my life."

"Probably shouldn't have given those pills on an empty stomach, huh?" Carolina slipped her hand into the crook of Hunt's arm and was thrilled when he gave it a reassuring squeeze. "How long do you think we'll be in jail for this?"

"Here comes Scruggs now. We can ask him."

As luck would have it, Officer Scruggs couldn't stay. Fine with Hunt. Scruggs said he was on his way to another call and he didn't have time to scrutinize the dogs' odd behaviors close up. Although, he did make some time to do a little scrutinizing of Carolina. The daily ice-cold drink was delivered along with a suggestive wink over the top of his mirrored sunglasses.

Jaw clamped, Hunt turned his back on their chatty conversation and feigned interest in the dogs' welfare. Anger seeped in to replace the peace and harmony he'd enjoyed earlier that day. He knew what Carolina was doing. And he knew why she was doing it.

Trouble was, she just didn't get it.

If anyone understood the highly competitive Eustace Scruggs, Jr., Hunt did. It didn't really matter *who* was out here serving time with Hunt. If there was a chance that Hunt might become interested, Scruggs would vie for her attention. Ever since Mary Helen Rogers, Scruggs had made it a point to move in on all single women within shouting distance of Hunt. Even though high school was over a decade behind them, the poor slob still had the need to prove to the people of Hidden Valley that he was "the man." Yep. Eustace was a textbook case in neuroses, but that didn't make it any easier on Hunt. Especially now that Scruggs had the gall to pick on a woman that Hunt actually—he ran a hand around the back of his neck and squeezed at the sharp pain there—cared about.

The man needed help.

And not the kind Carolina thought she could give.

Drawn by a shady patch under a tree, Hunt leaned against the trunk, his arms folded across his chest. Like bad reality TV, he had a hard time peeling his eyes away from the curbside freak show. Adoration tinged Scruggs's smile as Carolina tossed back her shimmering hair and emitted some musical laughter at some inane comment he'd murmured. Lightly she reached out and smacked Scruggs's hand, and he laughed.

Hunt's heart jumped around inside his chest like roosters in a cockfight. Wasn't there some rule against their cozy fraternizing? If there wasn't, there should be. She was supposed to be serving a sentence, for pity's sake. Instead she was trying to build self-esteem out of emotional quicksand. The muscles in the back of his jaw ached from the pressure it took to keep from shouting at Scruggs to move along. To leave Carolina alone and let her get back to work.

More laughter.

Light flirtation.

A giggle.

Okay. Enough was enough.

Itching to pick a fight, Hunt pushed off the tree trunk and stalked across the lawn just as Scruggs pulled away from the curb. He was lucky. This time.

"He was called to town on a domestic dispute," Carolina explained, watching the squad car turn out of sight.

"Yeah. Right." Good thing, considering the dispute

Hunt felt brewing with Scruggs. "You know, you really shouldn't spend so much time with him, unless you plan to go to bat on a romantic relationship."

"What? Me and Scruggs?" She turned to stare up at him, a frown of disbelief marring her flawless brow. "I don't want a romantic relationship with *him*."

"Then stop giving him that impression."

"What impression?"

"The impression that he's the funniest, hippest, hottest thing you ever laid eyes on."

"What on earth are you talking about? I simply laugh at the man's jokes and thank him for the occasional soda pop."

"You can't *do* that with a guy like Scruggs."

"Oh, please."

"Fine. Just don't act all surprised when he gets down on one knee and pops the question."

"What?" Carolina's laughter was incredulous. "That's crazy! He's just being friendly. I've explained all this to you before."

"Like it or not, I'm telling you the truth. He thinks you're coming on to him."

"I am *not* 'coming on' to Scruggs. I'm simply being nice. You're just jealous."

"Jealous?" Hunt's heart skipped a beat. Was he? Jealous? Of Scruggs? And more to the point, if he was truly jealous, did this mean that his aunt Rita was right and he'd fallen in love?

Yes.

There was no doubt about it. What an idiot. He'd fallen in love with Carolina Brubaker.

"Yes, jealous." She jammed her hands onto her hips. "You are all mad because every day he brings me a drink or something to eat and completely ignores you."

Hunt blinked. Something deep in his gut deflated, just a smidge.

"He simply appreciates being treated like a human being, and not some dorky reject from the forth-grade popular clique. I don't think he's ever really recovered from the way you guys used to treat him."

Hunt rolled his eyes. "Okay fine. While I appreciate that you've probably discussed this with your sister, the psychowizard, I know Scruggs. And he is seeing something in your conversations that you claim isn't there."

"He's not little Dragnet anymore, Hunt. He's a grown-up. And he's just being thoughtful. More than once he's hinted that because of my good behavior, he'd talk to his father on my behalf and see if he could get our sentence cut down. If you spent five minutes treating him civilly, you might see what I mean."

"If he was going to talk to his father, he'd have done it by now. Don't you get it? He likes having you around all summer to brighten his dreary days." Hunt laced his fingers behind his neck and arched back to release some of the tension he felt. "Come on. The dogs seem to be feeling better. Let's get 'em home.

As she concentrated on holding her leg steady, Carolina lay next to Georgia in the back row of an aerobics class in Hidden Valley's trendiest gym. Though they were supposed to be stretching after a vigorous workout, they chose to jabber instead of letting the tensions of the world fade away into the "white mists of contentment" exercise number three. At the moment Hunt was the focus of conversation.

"Do you think he's right?" Georgia grunted as she unsuccessfully tried to touch her forehead to her knees.

Carolina sighed as she bobbed and reached for her toes. "I don't know."

"You wanna know what I think?" Georgia fell back against her mat and stared at her sister with a knowing look.

"Hmm?"

"I think he's jealous."

"That's what I told him!" Carolina glanced around and lowered her voice. "I think he's mad because he thinks I get all of the snacks and ice cold drinks while he does all of the work."

Copying the instructor, Georgia changed positions. "No. That's not what I meant. I think he's jealous of *Scruggs*. I don't think Hunt likes it when you spend time flirting with the law."

Carolina snorted some unladylike laughter as the class focused on the "position of tranquility." "Hunt? Jealous of Scruggs? Ridiculous. Humanly impossible. And by the way, I'm not flirting. At least not the way… I—" She fell silent.

"The way you what?"

"Nothing."

"You were going to say 'the way I flirt with *Hunt*,' weren't you?"

Carolina felt the blood surge from her neck to her cheeks. "No." Hard as she tried, the usual tranquility eluded her.

After a minute, they rolled over onto their stomachs and grabbed their legs by the ankles and pulled up into the "peaceful rocking horse."

"What's going on between you two, anyway?" Her shoulder popped and Georgia winced in pain as she rocked.

"I don't know what you're talking about."

"Yes you do," she said. "You don't hate him anymore, do you? And he doesn't hate you!" Her eyes narrowed. "Are you and Hunt becoming an item?"

Carolina let go of her ankles and flopped out of position. She wasn't ready to discuss this. With anyone.

"You are, aren't you! Has he kissed you?"

She felt her cheeks flame impossibly brighter.

"He has, hasn't he!" Georgia let go of her ankles as paroxysms of uncontrollable laughter suddenly seized her. Knowing she shouldn't be laughing in class, but unable to control her hysteria, she slithered on her belly over the shiny hardwood floor and brought her nose to Carolina's so that she could speak privately.

"What's so funny? And would you kindly quit spitting in my face?"

Georgia had to battle to get the words out between fits of hilarity. "You…have to promise…not to get mad."

"Okay. I promise." Carolina's lips twitched.

"Today Brandon tried to kiss me—" Georgia covered her face and fell into another spasm of mirth "—and I hauled off and slapped him across the face with the beautiful bouquet he'd brought, because I thought you were still pining after him. There…were—" she clutched her sides and silently roared at the ceiling "—flower petals…everywhere…and he said…"

By this time Carolina was laughing as hard as her sister. She clutched a handful of Georgia's leotard. "What? Wha'd he say?"

"He said…'Your loyalty to your sister only makes me…love you more.' And so I let him have it again. Only the stems…were left."

"Ohhhh." Carolina and Georgia lay on the floor quaking with wild laughter. By now the entire class had abandoned the "stretch of serenity" to stare.

As the days of community service were crossed off the calendar, the weeks rolled one into the other. This particular Monday afternoon found Hunt and Carolina lounging, after a long day of road work, in one of Big Daddy's garden pavilions that he'd had built at the edge of a small lake behind their mansion.

Carolina loved this place. It was so incredibly beautiful here among the rich, well-manicured gardens. As far as the eye could see, there were sculptures and statues, fountains and pools, a maze of hedges, flower beds, Grecian-style outbuildings and walking paths that wound through thickly wooded hills. It was as close to Shangri-La as one could get here on this planet.

The open-air pavilion was shady and cool, and the thickly padded swing they shared was made for lazy comfort. Overhead, a ceiling fan stirred the air and a sweating jug of ice tea and a plate of sandwiches sat on a coffee table before them.

Carolina waved a bee away from her glass. "Did you do your homework?

"No. Did you?"

"No."

"Good. We can do it on the way to class tonight," Hunt said. He'd polished off his first sandwich and was reaching for a second.

"But I thought Mrs. Cullpepper said we were supposed to do this assignment alone."

"Why? Is Mrs. Cullpepper afraid I'm going to discover I have PMS if I copy your answers?"

Carolina pursed her lips. "I do not suffer from PMS."

"Right, right. And you don't snore, either."

"You know, someday I'm going to prove to you that I don't snore."

"You want us to sleep together? Now? I'm sorry, but that shocks me. But I'll get over it. Where would you like to begin? This is a nice place. A little public..." Grin goofy, he lifted a suggestive brow and patted the cushion beside him. "Little nappy? You and me? Right here?"

Carolina gasped and bit back some shocked laughter. "I did not say anything about sleeping with you."

"Too late. Already done that."

"I was in a different cell! You know, you are hopeless." Her heart pounding at the roguish look in his eye, Carolina forced herself to focus. "Homework. Put your sandwich down and open your book. We're going to get this over with now."

"Sure you don't want to spend some time convincing me you don't snore."

"No." Flipping through the pages of their *Healing the Angry Heart* manual, Carolina found this week's assignment, smoothed out the page and touched the end of her pencil to her tongue. "I'll write your answers on this side of the page, and mine on the other. Okay, it says here that we need to answer the following survey for discussion in class."

"Discussion? In *this* class? Mrs. Cullpepper is a dreamer, isn't she?" He reached for his glass and tossed back the remaining gulps of iced tea. "Okay, I'm ready. Hit me."

"Don't tempt me." Still smiling, Carolina read question one aloud. "'As far as you are able to tell, what is the general origin of your anger?'" She leaned against the back of the swing and tapped her eraser tip against her lower lip as she waited for him to give this some deep thought.

"You." He answered without hesitation.

"Me?"

"Yes. You."

The swing jostled as she turned to face him. "You mean to tell me, *I* am the source of *all* of your anger?"

"Pretty much, yeah."

She smirked. "You're kidding."

"No. Till I met you, I was a pretty laid-back guy."

"Laid-back. You." Carolina scrutinized his face. Was he serious? Or was he trying to push her buttons? She filled her lungs with air, closed her eyes and forced herself to envision her "happy place" as the material Mrs. Cullpepper had given them instructed she do whenever she felt irritated. "Okay." She scribbled her name as his answer as she wandered down the beach of her private island in her mind's eye. "That takes care of the first question for you. I'll answer mine in a second. Let's move along. Number two. 'What is your earliest anger-related memory?'"

"July 4, this year."

"Bull!" Carolina's eyes filled with suspicion.

"You callin' me a liar?"

"You mean to tell me you've *never* been mad before you met me."

"Never."

Humph. She scribbled July 4 into the allotted space. "Number three. What physical clues do you experience when you come in contact with your particular trigger?"

"Well, hmm." Taking his gaze off the squirrel he'd been watching, he eyed her up and down. "Well, you know, my heart pounds, my palms sweat, that kind of stuff. The blood flows to my extremities and I begin to feel…faint."

"When you're *angry.*"

"Yeah. Be sure to write that part down about my extremities. Then my face turns green and I bust out of my clothes and grow to twice my size—"

There was a teeny spasm at the edge of his lips. He was yanking her chain.

"You are so *full* of yourself."

Hunt threw back his head and roared as she scrubbed at his stupid answers with an eraser.

Anger management came and went in relative peace this session. The rest of the week progressed equally as calmly, and Thursday found Hunt and Carolina back at the police station.

"And so that's why I'm playing classical music to this one." Selma gestured to the headphones she had stretched across her bulging abdomen. "Not that my other kids are dumb or anything, but I read this article about 'womb learning' and thought it sounded like a good idea." She shrugged. "Couldn't hurt."

They were lounging behind the lobby desk of the Hidden Valley Municipal Building in rolling chairs with Selma, attempting to learn her complex and varied job while she prepared for maternity leave. Playing the receptionist for the police department, city hall, courthouse and jail, in a sleepy backwater like Hidden Valley was proving to be quite a challenge even after regular business hours. Selma had them come for lessons in the evenings, when she claimed it was slow. Easier to learn without so much hubbub, she'd said.

Even so, phones rang, radios squawked, people came and went, some forcibly, some of their own accord. Hunt couldn't imagine either himself or Carolina ever being able to fill Selma's sizable shoes in the evening, let alone in the busiest part of the day.

He glanced at Carolina and she seemed as flummoxed by it all as he was.

"When are you due?" Carolina asked during a rare quiet moment.

"Last week." Selma shot her a harried look. "All my kids are at least two weeks late and over ten pounds, so," she sighed, "we got time."

The phone rang.

"Okay. Punch up line one. Since that's the police department, you pick up the handset and say, "Hidden Valley Police Department, how may I direct your call?"

Hunt watched as Carolina punched up line one and then, panicking, handed the phone to him. He rolled his eyes. "Hidden Valley Police Department, how may I direct your call?"

The shrieking voice and the mayhem in the background had him toss the phone to Selma. She took the phone and calmly listened to the screaming. "You tell your sister I said you could. Yes. You tell her when I get home, heads are gonna roll. No, I am not kidding. Where's your father? What? Now? Why'd he go over there? Oh, for the love of— Listen, I'm gonna be home soon. You guys go put on your pajamas and brush your teeth. Yes, all six of you. Now! Put Aunt Sylvie on the phone."

The conversation continued until line two rang. And then line three.

"Hidden Valley Courthouse is closed for the day, may I take a message?"

"Hidden Valley City Hall, the…oh, hey, Judge! Yes, you do. One o'clock tomorrow. You're welcome."

Selma made it all look so easy. The people coming, going, asking questions, needing forms, wanting help. Finally the pandemonium wound down with the sun, and a bit of peace settled through the building.

Carolina slipped off her shoes and stretched. She was so tired.

With the exception of a security guard back in the jail and a couple of officers out on street patrol, everyone had gone home for the day.

Except them.

Selma grinned and then reared back in her chair for a

good stretch. "I know. It looks a…lot…harder than…
it is."

"You all right?" Hunt asked.

"Fine. Been sitting too long and my back is killing
me. I'd take some Tylenol, but I have to—" she raised
her voice and shouted at her belly "—wait until next
week."

Hunt glanced at Carolina. He'd have been happy to
tell Selma to go home and take a load off, but with Carolina clutching her pencil so tightly, he knew they
weren't ready. Thank God Selma wasn't leaving until
next week.

"You're not in labor, are you?" Carolina issued some
nervous laughter and drummed her eraser on the
counter top.

Concerned, Hunt's eyes flashed between the women.

Selma gave her hand an airy wave. "Ha. Don't I
wish. No, we'll *know* when I'm in labor. I get crushing
pains right around my belly button and they
squeeeeeze…oh, mercy. It's like being hit in the guts
by one of those big tractor-trailer rigs and then run over
and over and over until you have your little bundle of
joy."

"Oh?" Carolina was sorry she'd asked. However,
since it was quiet, Selma seemed to warm to the subject.

"And then my water breaks, always a pretty sight.
Usually when I'm at a party or some other social occasion. Completely ruins my dress. Not to mention the
upholstery."

"Sounds…lovely." Carolina's smile was more a gri-
mace. Medical stuff always left her feeling queasy.
Light-headed. Nauseated. She wished Selma would
stop with the graphic descriptions here.

"Yeah, last time I went into labor at church…ohhh,

mercy…which was lucky because everyone was praying up a storm that I could hang on until we got to the hospital. I did. Then, look out. The needles, the painkillers, the screaming, and that was just my husband."

The lights seemed to swim a little to Carolina.

Selma chuckled. "Since the second baby was born, I don't fool around. The last four have arrived within the hour." She shifted in her chair. "Ohhhhh…mercy."

"Back still hurt?" Hunt asked.

"Yeah. It seems to stop if I…ohhhhhhh mercy, change position."

"Maybe we should get you to a doctor?"

"Why? So they can send me home for another week. Noooooo thanks." A funny expression crossed Selma's face. "Uh-oh."

Both Hunt and Carolina glanced at Selma. "What, uh-oh?"

"Water broke."

Carolina dropped her head between her knees to keep from fainting.

Hunt stared, agog.

"But you said you were gonna wait until next week." Carolina's protests echoed off the floor between her shoes. Nobody ever said anything about broken water being part of her community service. She'd been through the absolute wringer with this whole paying-her-debt-to-society thing, but this was the limit.

"Sorry." Selma shrugged. "They never come this early."

Hunt jumped to his feet. "What now?"

"We go to the hospital. And, fast. I…feeeeeeeel…the urrrrrrge to pushhhhhh. Ohhhhhh, mercy." She doubled over and, clutching the placket of Hunt's shirt, groaned.

"Who should I call?" Hunt asked, glancing around for help.

Shaken and pasty, Carolina dragged her head from between her knees and looked up at him. "I have no idea. We are 911, aren't we?"

Selma clawed at his shirt. "We don't have time to chat with anyone, man. Get me to the hospital."

Taking charge, Hunt nodded at Carolina. "Let's go, I guess. I've got her." He swept the moaning Selma into his arms. "You go get the car."

"What? I can't go get the car." Stricken, Carolina clutched the front desk and swallowed the bile that rose in her throat. "I still don't know how to drive."

"No time like the present to learn."

Chapter Ten

"Where did you *park?*" Carolina blasted through the doors of the police station and felt frustration and fear well up in her throat like a tsunami swelling out at sea. Earlier that evening, Hunt had dropped her off here in front, so she had no idea where he'd left his SUV. Right now the only car in sight was Officer Scruggs's squad car. Since he was off duty, it was parked right in front of her, at the curb.

A groaning Selma in his arms, Hunt hurried through the double doors behind her. "My rig is behind the station."

"I have to puushhh."

"Oh, hell. Selma, honey, can I put you down?" Hunt tried setting the woman on her feet, but, seemingly in the throes of a contraction, she clutched his hair in a death grip. Stymied, he hiked Selma a little higher and nodded the squad car. "Open the door."

"But we can't drive this car, we don't have the keys—"

"Just *open the door!*"

Yes. Selma needed a place to have her baby. Now. Carolina nodded and turned in a panicked circle. The car was right there. Excellent idea. She stumbled to the back door and yanked it open. A foul stench filled the air and several soda cans fell out and clattered to the ground.

With great care, Hunt moved to the back passenger area and lowered a heavily breathing Selma to the seat. "Selma honey? I'm just going to help you into the car and then we'll get you to the—"

"Nooo!" Her fingers frozen to his hair, Selma fell back onto the seat, taking Hunt with her in the process. "Don't leave me! The baby…the baby…the *baby is coming!"*

"Uh…I…" He tossed a frantic look over his shoulder at Carolina. "Go inside and see if you can find the keys."

"Top drawer…Scruggs's…desssk."

On the wings of terror, Carolina flew into the station, found the keys and shot back out to the squad car. Breathless, she held them out to Hunt. "Here you go."

"You drive."

Her jaw dropped. "No way! You know what will happen if I drive, and besides, I've never driven this car—"

"Drive!"

Selma had Hunt in a mortal headlock.

Okay. He couldn't drive with a pregnant woman around his neck. Carolina clutched the keys. But—she tried to swallow past the tumbleweed that was suddenly her tongue—she'd never driven a car like this. Especially after sunset. As she peered at the confusing dash, she felt the panic rise and wanted to scream. What if she couldn't get the engine started? And this was a police car, for heaven's sake. Shouldn't it be automatic? Then again, in Hidden Valley, nothing was ever up-to-date.

From the back seat, Selma moaned and Hunt murmured soothing platitudes. What if she killed the engine, or worse...*them?* Her heart throbbed in her throat and she felt light-headed as she thought of her responsibility to the tiny babe. No way could she do this. She didn't function well in emergencies. That's what household staff was for. That's it. She should call Basil.

"Carolina." Hunt's voice seemed to come from far, far away. "Drive."

Right. This was no time to be a Dresden doll. Remnants of her fight with Brandon echoed. Mechanically she climbed into the front seat. With a deep, steadying breath, she inserted the key into the ignition, depressed the clutch and with a prayer and a flick of her wrist, the engine roared to life. Oh, thank God. She pushed the hair from her face and after adjusting her mirror shouted, "Seat belts!"

The engine rumbled. Behind her, Selma moaned. Like it or not, the rest was up to Carolina.

"First gear," she murmured. Jaw set, she grabbed hold of the stick, depressed the clutch and closed her eyes. The car lurched forward, and they were off. Sort of. In her haste to release the clutch, she killed the engine. Once she had it restarted, she found first, jumped on the gas and bumped over the curb and into the street.

Selma groaned.

"Sorry." Out on the main road, Carolina grasped the wheel and headed toward town.

"Check the odometer," Hunt instructed from the back seat. "You're past ten heading to twenty."

"Twenty?" Selma moaned. "Ten is fully dilated."

"No. I mean Carolina." He nodded at Selma. "You, breathe."

"You talkin' to me?" Carolina wondered which of the

dials before her could be an odometer. And, when she found it, what good would it do her?

"No, Selma."

"Whaaaaat?"

At the pain in Selma's voice, Carolina pressed a little harder on the gas and after a quick check of oncoming traffic, decided it was safe to pass the van from the senior center that crawled down the road before them. Beads of sweat popped out on her upper lip and forehead and her entire body seemed to shimmy along with the car. She came alongside the van. Milton was driving. Carolina waved.

Confused, Milton waved back.

Still in Selma's clutches, Hunt rolled the window down, and a gust of fresh air swirled into the cab. Carolina filled her lungs and began to relax until Hunt started to fling garbage out the window.

"Hey! Quit that!" In her rearview mirror, she could see Milton careening about, his windshield wipers working overtime to deal with the foul deluge. "We're just gonna have to pick all that up! Plus we'll *really* be in trouble. You know how the judge hates litter." She had to shout to be heard over the screaming engine. It sounded as if she was driving a rocket, but strangely they were only crawling.

"Right now *you're* the law. Besides, the baby will need a tetanus shot if we don't get rid of some of this moldy, rusty junk. And by the way, *shift* already." Hunt tossed out another load of trash and it fluttered to the four winds.

"But what if I kill the engine?"

"The way you're going, it'll be dead long before we get to the hospital. You can do this." Hunt's voice was soothing.

"I can?"

"Yes…I can…" Selma panted.

"Smoke." Carolina pointed out the windshield. "The engine is smoking."

Selma moaned.

"Listen to me," Hunt said.

"Me?" Carolina asked.

"No," Hunt said. "*Hoo…hoo…hee.* Good girl. You're going to hyperventilate if you don't breathe."

"Okay. *Hoo…hoo…hee,*" Carolina murmured.

"Ease off the gas."

"Me?" Selma wondered with a frown.

"Carolina. Push in the clutch. Right. Now, shift into second."

The screeches of a wood chipper decimating a tree branch filled the air as Carolina searched for the proper gear. Dumb luck was on her side and, as she switched pedals, the car surged forward, throwing them all back against the seats. "Hang on!" She stomped on the accelerator.

"I hope the baby doesn't get whiplash," Selma moaned and clutched her belly.

"Breathe," Hunt urged.

Again the engine screamed. So did Selma. And Carolina.

"Carolina, it's time for third gear."

"Already? But I *just did* that."

"I gotta pushhh."

"Just do it." Hunt tossed a box of stale crullers out the window.

Knuckles white, Carolina gripped the wheel with one hand and the gear shift with another. The nerve-racking cacophony of grating metal sounded once more as she found the proper gear. Jaw set with determination, she blazed through an oncoming red light at a busy intersection. Cars swerved and skidded to avoid collision, and she mopped her brow with her sleeve.

Darting a glance over her shoulder, she asked, "How we doin'?"

"Hanging in there." Hunt's voice was muffled as Selma yanked him through another contraction. "Uh, can we go a little faster?"

"I can try, but I think I'm already breaking land-speed records in this heap." Rubber burned as she took another corner, and the Kojak light bounced into her lap.

She contemplated her actions for a moment before she rolled down her window, clapped the suction light onto the roof and flipped the switch as she'd seen Scruggs do on more than one occasion. On the dash she found the siren button, and the wails vied with Selma for decibel supremacy. Heady with her success, Carolina stabbed at the clutch and threw the car into reverse.

Oops. Momentary setback.

After a bit of grinding, they were finally in fourth and flying. Cars on both sides of the road pulled over and let them pass as Carolina barreled toward the hospital. No wonder Scruggs loved his job. This, was *great.*

"That's my girl." There was pride in Hunt's low voice.

"Me?" Selma grunted.

"No." Carolina grinned. "Me."

"Kinda makes me want one of my own," Hunt said.

"It does?" Carolina's sharp exhale fogged the nursery window as they stood together in the maternity ward, peering at Selma's tiny baby.

"Mmm. Of course, I'd want her to look just like you."

Carolina dared not move. Her high voice, when she finally found it, was an embarrassment. "Like me?" What did he mean?

"I bet you were a beautiful baby."

"If you like that pointy-head look."

Hunt chuckled. "Look at her. She's so...tiny. Dependant. Makes you want to protect her from the big bad world."

"You did a great job tonight."

Hunt slipped his arm around her waist. "No. Tonight you were the hero. I've never been so proud of anyone in all my life."

Carolina raised smiling lips to capture his kiss.

Baby Girl Featherstone had graciously waited until her mother reached the hospital before making her appearance. However, she hadn't been so considerate of her father, who had still been on his way. Since Selma had seemed incapable—and profoundly unwilling—to release Hunt's hair, he and Carolina had coached Selma through the birth.

When the baby was born, Carolina had held her hands over her mouth and cried. And laughed. And cried even harder. And though Hunt was smiling, there were tears coursing down his cheeks, too. It was incredible. Moving. Nearly holy in its beauty. As she'd blubbered with joy, Hunt had wrapped her in his arms and given her a congratulatory kiss that had Carolina convinced that there was something serious behind the action.

Before they'd left the birthing room, Selma let them both hold the baby and they'd counted her tiny fingers and toes and marveled over the miracle of life. It was an intensely awesome and bonding moment that Carolina would never forget.

Eventually they followed the baby to the nursery, where they couldn't seem to pry themselves away from the window and go home for some much-needed rest.

"Now, that's what I call teamwork." Judge Scruggs hovered behind Carolina and Hunt as they stood, locked in a private embrace that said they'd forgotten the rest of the world.

"Yep." The judge put his hands on their backs and urged them to turn around. "She's a little beauty."

Hunt cleared his throat. "Hey, Judge."

"I hear you two did a remarkable thing together this evenin'. In fact—" the judge removed his glasses and polished the oversize lenses as he spoke "—in light of your heroism tonight, I have decided to commute the rest of your sentence, if you will both simply give the widow Foster a hand in her garden tomorrow. We've got a temp that can cover for Selma."

Dumbfounded, Carolina stared. She was off the hook? No more community service? No more sweltering days in the hot sun, picking up garbage and chasing kids and dogs? A strange lump surged into her throat. She should be jumping for joy, but instead she felt oddly blue.

She glanced at Hunt and forced a smile. Time seemed to suspend as their eyes met. His expression was inscrutable, and Carolina wondered if he was happy. Now he could go back to work. Get back to his real life. And she...hers.

"Oh. That's...great," Carolina said.

"I knew you would be pleased. And after the way the two of you pulled together tonight, there is no doubt in my mind that you have both learned the lessons put forth by the court." The judge rubbed the stem of his specs against his jaw. "I have to tell you I didn't hold out much for you two as a team."

"Thank you." She knew the feeling.

Hunt only nodded.

"I'm pleasantly surprised." The judge held out his hand. "Congratulations on a job well done. Good luck to you both in the future."

Their final day of community service took them back to the scene of their arrest. The widow Foster was a bright-eyed little wisp of a woman with a face that looked as if it had been carved from a shriveled apple. Like a hummingbird, she never really seemed to land anywhere for more than a moment before she'd flit off to another flower or shrub and give a dissertation on its origin. Considering her advanced years, her energy was boundless, and after a morning spent working with this master gardener, Carolina was exhausted.

The scientific names, the common names, the anecdotes and horticulture lessons were more than Carolina could digest in only one day, but they were nothing compared to the physical labor. Needing a break, she limped to the porch and fell onto the steps. Already that morning, they'd weeded, fertilized, mowed, pruned, clipped and put the gnome garden back to rights.

With a sigh, Carolina pushed herself upright and poured an ice-cold glass of raspberry lemonade from the pitcher on the porch. As she sipped, she watched the sweet interaction between Hunt and the widow. As the tiny woman outlined her "vision" for the flamingo corner, he bent low and patiently listened.

Carolina's heart swelled and her chest grew tight. Such a lovely man. How could she ever have thought otherwise? Pinpricks of guilt niggled. She'd never made the effort to see past the stereotype. Well, never again.

Clasping her hands together around her knees, she made her decision.

Today was the day. After work, she was going to tell Hunt how she'd fallen in love with him. There was no way she could hold it in anymore. If he didn't feel the same, well, that was a chance she was willing—and yet terrified—to take.

She gnawed her lower lip. What if he still saw her as unworthy of serious involvement? She didn't want to think about that. She would simply continue to prove otherwise. Until she was as old as the widow Foster, if that's what it took.

There was a tiny palsy in the widow's hand as she shaded her eyes from the sun. Carolina loved the way Hunt made slipping his arm through hers look chummy, rather than simply to keep the teetering woman from falling down. Though the widow would never admit it, it had been a long, hard morning, and she needed a rest.

Carolina poured a second glass of lemonade and beckoned the older woman to join her on the steps. The widow nodded and shuffled over. She perched at the edge of a step and, after several sips of her drink, turned to face Carolina.

"You are a very lucky young woman."

"Me? How so?"

"He's a wonderful man to work with."

"Mmm." Carolina's gaze strayed to Hunt. "That, he is."

"Puts me in mind of my Bernard. Hardworking, sweet, generous, funny and—" Widow Foster's tremor had the liquid in her glass sloshing a bit "—completely 'hot' as the kids say today."

Having just taken a big gulp of lemonade, Carolina had to force herself to swallow around an explosion of laughter. She coughed and choked. "Hot?"

"Yes," the widow Foster mused. "He's a hottie. Take a gander at that bod. Talk about your muscles. Ooo*wee!*" She gave her knee an appreciative slapping.

Eyes wide, lips slack, Carolina stared at the woman at her side.

"What?" The little woman blinked in innocence. "Look at him, kid! All of the Boy Scout virtues packaged into Michelangelo's *David*. Now there's a treasure more precious than gold. Don't let that slip away simply because this is your last day of work together and you're rich and he's not. Don't let that silly class-distinction stuff hinder you. Is it? Hindering you?"

"Actually, no—"

"Good! If I was you, I'd nab him today. Before some other gal gets her hooks in him."

"You would?"

"Of course. What are you waiting for? You two are lovely together. Pity. Your children will be ugly. It's always that way with beautiful people, I'm sorry to say."

"Today?" Carolina cleared her throat. "You'd nab him today?" Was this some kind of sign?

"It's time to fish or cut bait, honey. He is twice the man Brandon McGraw ever *thought* of being."

"You…know about Brandon?"

"Dearie—" Widow Foster patted Carolina's hand "—everyone knows about Brandon. This is a small town. What we don't learn from Jasper and Scooter in the *Gazette,* we hear over the back fence. Oh, Hunt!" The widow watched as Hunt finished digging a series of holes for her bedding plants. "Honey, get out of that heat. We have cookies and lemonade up here for you. You can wash up in the kitchen."

"Okay." Tossing his shovel aside, Hunt picked up his T-shirt, dusted off his hands, stretched and then headed toward the porch.

Widow Foster leaned closer to Carolina and continued her advice after the screen door had slammed shut behind Hunt. "Anyway, if you don't mind a little interference from an old lady, you'll tell your little sister to dump that Brandon chump before things get serious."

"I…" Completely nonplussed, Carolina pressed her hands to her scalding cheeks. The entire town knew her business.

"Oh, nuts." The widow Foster harrumphed and set

her glass on the porch and she glowered down the street. "Dragnet's coming. Something about that show-off sets my teeth on edge."

"Officer Scruggs? I think he means well enough, it's just that his self-esteem—"

"Oh, don't give me your sister's psychobabble. He's an idiot."

Officer Scruggs swung the squad car up to the curb and parked. He emerged from the driver's seat carrying a bouquet of flowers and, spotting Carolina on the steps, moved toward the porch. He propped a chunky shoe on the first step.

"Good morning, ladies."

Widow Foster sniffed. "Morning, Eustace."

Carolina smiled. "Hello, Officer Scruggs."

"I hear you had a little excitement last night."

"Yes, we did."

"Yes. You sure did. Yes. You did. Indeed. Sure enough." Nervous laughter filled the time as he groped for more conversation. "*Ohh,* yeah." The ensuing silence was thicker than day-old mush. "Oh, and I also hear congratulations are in order. This is your last day of community service." With a little bow, he handed Carolina the flowers he'd brought. "For you, milady."

"Oh, I…why…look, Mrs. Foster! Aren't they beautiful?"

The widow's lips pruned.

"Thank you. They're beautiful, Officer Scruggs."

"Call me Eustace. I'm not your boss anymore."

"Okay. Eustace."

The familiar mottled patches of heat crawled up Officer Scruggs's neck and over his face. Hands in his pockets, he rocked back and forth and fidgeted with the coins and keys in his pocket. "I…I…" He swallowed.

"Considering this is your last day and all, how about you let me take you out for supper? To celebrate. My treat."

He looked so hopeful and vulnerable and mottled and…sweaty. Carolina could almost see a sixth-grader standing there, staring wistfully at Mary Helen Rogers. It was so sad.

Caught off guard and by complete surprise, Carolina searched the recesses of her spinning brain for an excuse that wouldn't embarrass anyone. Or even an embarrassing excuse, if it didn't hurt anyone. In fact, *any* plausible excuse would do the trick.

But there was none.

She honestly had nothing written on her calendar that evening and was at a complete loss for a cover story. What should she say?

She didn't want to go out with Scruggs. She wanted to go out with Hunt. To celebrate their freedom. To tell him that she loved him. And to, hopefully, hear those very words from him. But she hadn't gotten around to asking, and Scruggs had beaten her to the punch. Damn.

Damn.

Double damn.

The sweat was pouring down the sides of Scruggs's face now, and he looked like a cat at the dog pound. "I…was thinking you might…uh…enjoy some barbecue and a few beers down at the Jubilee Truck Stop. They have great live music. And—" he chuckled "—you do owe me a favor."

Yeah. A vision of his mangled truck flashed through her mind. He had mentioned that favor thing, hadn't he?

A few weeks ago the old Carolina could have brushed him off without a lot of guilt. But not anymore. These days she went the extra mile to see the person inside, and not simply judge the quality of the book by its rather confusing, and sometimes inexpensive, cover.

Shoulders flagging, she guessed sharing a rib or two with Scruggs was the least she could do. Unable to take another second of his shuffling embarrassment, she put him out of his misery. "Ribs sound very nice. Perhaps we could meet at the, er, truck stop? Around say—" Never? "—seven?" There. Two hours and it would all be over.

If Hunt was right and Scruggs had somehow gotten the wrong idea about the two of them, she could set him straight. Over…ribs. After that she could—in clear conscience—call Hunt and ask him out.

Scruggs inhaled his excitement, spun around and, completely forgetting to bid them good day, loped to his car.

As the officer drove off, Hunt nudged open the screen door and emerged from the house.

He looked at Carolina for a long, silent moment. The accusations, though unspoken, were plain. With a nod at Widow Foster, Hunt took the porch steps two at a time and stalked back to the flamingo bed and set to work.

How could she explain?

Panic closed her throat and made enlightening him impossible. She'd been too spineless to stand up to the officer and tell him that there was someone else in her life. And, at the same time, she'd managed to prove to Hunt that she was still using Scruggs to garner some kind of special favor with the law.

He thought she was a perennial user, and she was no doubt using him right along with everyone else in her path.

Chapter Eleven

That evening Hunt spent a miserable dinner hour over at Colt and Ginny's pushing his food around his plate and glancing at their slowly ticking clock. The couple had exchanged many worried looks during the course of the meal, but until now, had avoided the subject of Carolina and her date with Officer Scruggs.

Finally Ginny could stand the tension no longer. "Hunt, honey."

Startled from his reverie, Hunt jerked his head up from where he'd been staring at his plate, and focused a bleary gaze on Carolina's sister. "Mmm?"

"When I was a very little girl, Big Daddy had a litter of barn cats."

Hunt shrugged and sighed. He was in no mood for a trip down memory lane, but he guessed he didn't have much choice at this juncture.

"Anyway, there was a runt. So skinny it looked like a pair of eyeballs with legs. Its tail was broken in three places, and it meowed constantly."

Propping his cheek in his hand, Hunt glanced at Colt. Was this some kind of analogy? Did she see him as a runt? Colt shrugged and nodded for him to keep listening.

"Every day, Carolina would go to the barn and hold this little cat. When it became clear that the poor thing wasn't eating, she got an eye dropper and some baby formula, and nursed the stupid thing until it was huge. And grumpy. And selfish. And meaner than a junkyard dog. She's still got a couple of scars from that thing. Just couldn't seem to let go of a lost cause. Some folks are like that."

Ginny stopped talking and moved to the coffeepot and fussed with the filter and grounds.

Hunt sat there, stunned, as the true meaning of her story dawned. Pushing back his chair, he jumped to his feet and moved to the door. Colt was hot on his heels.

"I'll just see you boys later," Ginny said, and began to clear the dishes.

Within moments Hunt was on his way to the Jubilee Truck Stop with Colt to catch him a bad cat.

Clearly, this nutty woman needed protection from herself, and doggone it, it looked like he was elected. Not that he would have been able to stay away, but this was hardly the way he'd envisioned spending this, the last evening of his community service. Then again, since he'd been slow to ask Carolina out, he could hardly blame Scruggs for asking a beautiful woman to join him for dinner.

But he didn't have to like the fact that she'd said yes.

Yes.

Dammit anyway. Why had she said yes? Clearly, he'd mistaken her chatty, sunny nature as a weapon she employed to get her way.

But he'd been wrong.

All along.

Ever since the day he'd first set eyes on her one summer back in high school. He'd watched her cavort with her silly, giggly, upper-crust cronies, while he'd still been trying to deal with the depression and grief of having lost his mother.

So he'd judged her through jaded eyes. And he was still doing it today. And it wasn't fair. To her. To him. To anyone who was drawn to her by her sense of humor and drama and compassion.

All of these were the reasons he'd fallen in love with her, but for the love of Mike, couldn't she, just once, have a little backbone? Especially in this instance.

He'd wanted to take her out tonight. *He'd* been planning a special evening, just the two of them at a cozy restaurant, where he planned to tell her how he felt. That he'd fallen in love with her and hoped that she felt the same.

Now he knew that she'd been ambushed by Dragnet and was only being polite. He should have known better. He'd been witness to Scruggs's shy, vulnerable act all through grade school. Trouble was, being polite to Scruggs was just that. Trouble. The spoiled creep would never be able to take no for an answer. No doubt that's why he'd become a cop. People generally didn't say no to him these days. Unless they wanted to end up at the Gray Bar.

"You sure you want to go through with this?" Colt asked as Hunt pulled into the truck stop's parking lot. The live music filtered out of the building along with the mouthwatering aroma of ribs smoking on the pit.

"With what?"

"This. Spying on Scruggs and Carolina?"

"Hell, yes." Hunt jumped out of his rig and slammed

his door. "You remember that weenie back in high school. I think he invented stalking."

"Yeah, but he never hurt anybody."

"Yet. There's always a first time for everything. C'mon." Using his remote, Hunt shot the locks of his SUV and, with Colt right behind him, moved through the gathering throng to the interior of the popular Jubilee. Once he got used to the dim, smoke-filled lounge, he spotted Carolina.

And Scruggs.

Looked like Scruggs's face was even more florid than ever and there was a looseness about him that had nothing to do with his usual stone-cold sobriety. One at a time, Hunt cracked his knuckles. No way was he letting that greaseball drive Carolina home. If he had to, he'd make a citizen's arrest. He glanced at Colt, who seemed equally concerned and mouthed, "He's been drinking."

Colt nodded.

Moving behind the crowd, they stood together and watched. Somehow, Scruggs had persuaded Carolina to join him out on the dance floor for a slow dance. He'd taken the languid rhythm of the music as permission to hold Carolina close and let his hands do a little roving. It was clear Carolina was more than a little busy staving off his advances and keeping a respectable distance between their bodies.

Colt inclined his head toward an empty table in an out-of-the-way corner. Reluctantly Hunt joined him. When they were settled, they ordered coffee.

"Now don't do anything stupid." Colt had to raise his voice to be heard above the band.

"Me? I'm not the idiot here."

Colt lifted and dropped a shoulder. "True enough. But remember, he's the guy with the badge. And—" there was a rueful twist to his lips "—the gun."

"I'm not afraid of Scruggs." Jaw set, heart pounding, Hunt forced himself to remain calm. And seated. But it was the toughest thing he'd ever done.

"I was really, really, really—" Scruggs paused and frowned as he lost his train of thought. "Oh, yeah. Really, really, really nervous to go out with you."

Carolina issued some stilted laughter. How was she going to convince Scruggs that they were all wrong for each other when she was reasonably sure he'd have no recollection of anything she said tonight? Trying to smile, she grabbed his hands and yanked. "No, no, no, Officer Scruggs. Please keep your hands up on my waist."

"My pleasure." His hands dipped again. "But, you know you owe me a purty big ol' favor." He pressed his grin into her neck and belched. "That truck was bran' new. 'Ss payback time."

The fumes alone told Carolina that he'd spent some considerable time bellied up to the bar and calming his nerves, long before she'd arrived that night.

"So." Scruggs reared back and, his bloodshot eyes swimming, peered into Carolina's face. "Marry me?"

From where Hunt sat, he watched Officer Scruggs move, almost as if in a trance. And, when Carolina tried to push him away, he only pulled her closer, planting his searching, slobbering mouth on her jaw. Her cheek. Her lips.

"No!" Exasperated, Carolina arched back and planted her hands firmly against his chest. "Please. You are going to have to stop it, Eustace!"

"Okay." Seemingly caught up in his own fantasy world, Eustace couldn't hear her. Or didn't want to.

Hunt pushed himself to his feet and sighed. "Time to cut in." He beckoned Colt, who, with a supportive nod, followed him to the dance floor. "You take care of your sister-in-law. I want to talk to Scruggs."

The look of relief in Carolina's eyes when she spotted him standing with Colt at the edge of the dance floor was satisfying but Hunt had decided to let her stew in her juices for a while. He gave her a curt nod of acknowledgment, but nothing more. He'd deal with her later. When he'd had a chance to calm down.

Hunt strode over to tap Scruggs on the shoulder. "May I?"

Scruggs blinked up at him in heavy-lidded surprise. "I don' want to dance with you."

"Good. That makes my job a little easier." Hunt grabbed a fistful of the officer's shirt with one hand and delivered a clean right cross to the jaw with the other. That's when the screaming started and the music died. In the sudden silence that ensued, the crowd's collective gasp echoed.

Rubbing his hand, Hunt took a step back and leveled his gaze at the bleeding Scruggs. "That was for Mary Helen Rogers. And every other woman you've hassled over the years."

Horrified, Carolina rushed to Scruggs's side and dropped to her knees. "Hunt." She moaned as she dabbed at the blood with the hem of her skirt. "You shouldn't have done this."

Unfortunately, two officers from the county sheriff's department had seen the whole thing and had to agree with her assessment.

"Guess not," Hunt admitted as the officers slapped a set of cuffs on his wrists and escorted him through the staring crowd to their waiting squad car. "But it was worth it."

Head bent, he was shoved into the back seat. Hunt sighed. It was déjà vu all over again.

* * *

Alone in his jail cell with his back to the door, Hunt refused to turn around, let alone acknowledge Carolina's existence. She blinked back the idiotic tears that threatened. Though she'd done her best for a good half hour to explain that it was her fear for Hunt that had her rushing to see if Scruggs was alive, and not any feelings for her drunken date, it was no use. Clearly, he had no intention of forgiving her. He was silent, save for the angry popping of his gum.

Humiliated for the last time, Carolina pushed off the bars and moved slowly down the hall and out of the jail. The attending guard closed the door behind her and, keys jangling, locked the door.

Once she reached the area where her brother-in-law waited, she fell into his arms and cried until his shirt was soaked.

"I know," Colt murmured. "He can be a stubborn cuss."

Mutely Carolina nodded.

"If you're ready, I'll take you home."

"No. Instead, would you please take me to the widow Foster?"

Since Carolina had left, the hours had crawled by and Hunt lay on his bed feeling lower than a run-over worm in a ditch. His sore punching hand tucked under his armpit, he stared at the ceiling and decided that the only silver lining in this whole crap-sandwich day was the fact that Scruggs was in the emergency room with a broken jaw. And he'd have taken real satisfaction in that, if he hadn't just blown his future with Carolina.

What would a woman like her ever see in a hot-tempered loser like him?

Nothing.

So, it was best to cut his losses now, before his heart was as bloodied and bruised as his fist.

Nearly twenty-four hours passed in miserable fits of sleep and regret. Then, just when he thought he'd been forgotten like yesterday's news, the distant sounds of a brouhaha out in the police station lobby had his eyes sliding open.

Minutes later, keys jangled in the now-familiar series of locks. Judge Scruggs entered holding a tray with a huge, rather lopsided, two-layer chocolate cake, two plates, two forks, two cups and a thermos. Upon letting himself into Hunt's cell, Judge Scruggs set the cake down and motioned for Hunt to sit up.

"Carolina Brubaker brought us a cake. And she was pretty insistent that we have a slice."

"What?" A cake? Hunt swung his legs to the floor. Damnation, what on earth would Carolina think up next?

As the judge sliced into the cake, he paused and peered through his lenses at the lumpy chocolate mess. Reaching into the cake with two fingers, he retrieved a standard-size piece of…cardboard. "What the devil is this?"

Tilting his head, Hunt frowned. "Looks like a file."

"Yeah, but it's a manila file folder. Hardly useful for busting outta here."

Hunt snorted. "Trust Carolina to bake the wrong kind of a file into my cake."

With a shrug, the judge handed the folder to Hunt and turned back to the business of slicing them pieces of cake.

Hunt opened the folder, found a note and began to read aloud.

My dear Hunt:
    I spoke with Mrs. Foster, who seems to think that you love me. That you are in love with me, the way her Barney was with her. I'm hoping that

she is right, because I love you, too. Please forgive me for being such a pain this summer. You helped me to grow up, and have taught me so much about maturity and responsibility and kindness and caring.

And love.

I want to spend the rest of my life with you.

If you feel the way I do, would you please hand this card to Judge Scruggs and ask him to marry us at his earliest convenience.

I love you,

Carolina

Hunt lifted a 'Get Out of Jail Free' Monopoly card off the page.

Carolina waited with bated breath in the lobby. What if her plan didn't work? What if the widow Foster was wrong? What if Hunt didn't love her enough to marry her? Her mouth was so dry. She turned to the cooler and slugged down several Dixie cups full of water. The waiting was unbearable. She was shaking like an Oscar nominee.

If the answer was yes, what on earth was taking so long?

She glanced at the clock. Then at the widow Foster. The old woman gave her an encouraging nod, but Carolina's heart began to sink.

He wasn't coming.

Tears in her eyes, she turned to go, but something stopped her. Distant footsteps sounded from the jail area and finally the door swung open.

Hunt!

He emerged, a broad smile on his face. Her heart stopped, and without waiting for it to start again she flew at him, landed in his arms and kissed him as if there was no tomorrow. The widow Foster stood off to the side with Ginny and of course Colt, Georgia, Big Daddy, Miss Clarise, Uncle Mike and Aunt Rita.

"I love you," Hunt murmured, and kissed her again. "And, yes. I want to marry you. Here. Now. Will you still have me?"

"Yes! Oh, Hunt. I love you so much."

"I've been such an idiot—"

"I've been so worried—"

"I'm so sorry about everything. I was wrong to misjudge you—"

"No, you're not an idiot. I'm the spoiled brat—"

"—and stereotype you. You are the sweetest—"

"Oh, Hunt, no, really—"

"Dammit woman! Do you ever shut those flapping lips?"

Carolina smiled. "Sometimes."

Hunt pushed her mouth into place with his lips, and they kissed until Judge Scruggs appeared and cleared his throat.

"If we're gonna do this, let's get on with it. I've had your paperwork rushed through the proper channels. Everything's in order. Just need a couple of signatures and 'I do's'. C'mon." He beckoned for the group to follow him. "The cake's back here. And it's delicious."

When they reached Hunt's cell, the judge had the audience make themselves comfortable on and beside the bed, and then strode to stand in front of the commode and faced the couple.

"Hunt, I've watched you grow from a young boy into a fine man. I only wish my own son had some of your great qualities. But he's learning, I guess." His eyes misty, the judge turned to Carolina. "And, Carolina, I've watched you grow up, too, only on a different timetable and in different ways. You are a lovely, caring and generous young woman, and it took a good man like Hunt to make those qualities shine in you."

The widow Foster shared her box of tissues with Big Daddy as Hunt and Carolina repeated their vows and publicly declared to love each other until death parted them, and beyond.

When the all-too-brief ceremony was over, they fed each other pieces of chocolate cake, and posed for Scooter, who insisted they have top billing on the society page. One at a time the guests wished them well, polished off a bit of cake and left.

Keys jangling, Judge Scruggs locked them in their cell, turned out the lights and, just before he closed the door, promised to let them free in the morning.

They didn't even notice.

* * * * *

So now that Georgia is dating Brandon, what wild adventure is she going to be involved in? Find out next month in Carolyn Zane's

GEORGIA GETS HER GROOM!

(Hint: the groom isn't who you think!)

Receive a FREE hardcover book from

H A R L E Q U I N   R O M A N C E ®

in September!

Harlequin Romance celebrates the launch of the line's new cover design by offering you this exclusive offer valid only in September, only in Harlequin Romance.

To receive your FREE HARDCOVER BOOK written by bestselling author Emilie Richards, send us four proofs of purchase from any September 2004 Harlequin Romance books. Further details and proofs of purchase can be found in all September 2004 Harlequin Romance books.

Must be postmarked no later than October 31.

Don't forget to be one of the first to pick up a copy of the new-look Harlequin Romance novels in September!

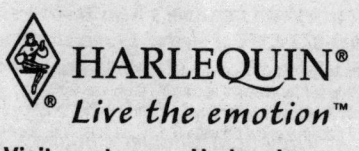

HARLEQUIN®
Live the emotion™

Visit us at www.eHarlequin.com

HRPOP0904

If you enjoyed what you just read,
then we've got an offer you can't resist!

Take 2 bestselling love stories FREE!

Plus get a FREE surprise gift!

The *New York Times* bestselling author of
16 Lighthouse Road and *311 Pelican Court*
welcomes you back to Cedar Cove,
where life and love is anything but ordinary!

DEBBIE MACOMBER

Dear Reader,

I love living in Cedar Cove, but things just haven't been the same since Max Russell died in our B and B. We still don't have any idea why he came here and—most important of all—who poisoned him!

But we're not providing the only news in town. I heard that Maryellen Sherman is getting married and her mother, Grace, has her pick of interested men—but which one will she choose? And Olivia Griffin is back from her honeymoon, and her mother, Charlotte, has a man in her life, too, but I'm not sure Olivia's too pleased....

There's plenty of other gossip I could tell you. Come by for a cup of tea and one of my blueberry muffins and we'll talk.

44 Cranberry Point

"Macomber is known for her honest portrayals of
ordinary women in small-town America, and this tale
cements her position as an icon of the genre."

—*Publishers Weekly* on *16 Lighthouse Road*

*Available the first week of September 2004,
wherever paperbacks are sold.*

On sale now

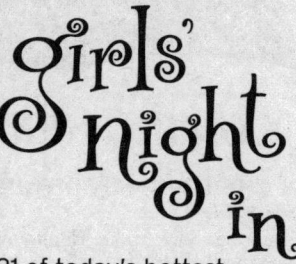

girls' night in

21 of today's hottest
female authors
1 fabulous short-story collection
And all for a good cause.

Featuring *New York Times* bestselling authors

Jennifer Weiner (author of *Good in Bed*),
Sophie Kinsella (author of *Confessions of a Shopaholic*),
Meg Cabot (author of *The Princess Diaries*)

Net proceeds to benefit War Child, a network of organizations
dedicated to helping children affected by war.

Also featuring bestselling authors...

Carole Matthews, Sarah Mlynowski, Isabel Wolff, Lynda Curnyn,
Chris Manby, Alisa Valdes-Rodriguez, Jill A. Davis, Megan McCafferty,
Emily Barr, Jessica Adams, Lisa Jewell, Lauren Henderson,
Stella Duffy, Jenny Colgan, Anna Maxted, Adèle Lang,
Marian Keyes and Louise Bagshawe

www.RedDressInk.com   www.WarChildusa.org

Available wherever trade paperbacks are sold.

™ is a trademark of the publisher.
The War Child logo is the registered trademark of War Child.

RDIGNIMMR

SILHOUETTE *Romance*®

COMING NEXT MONTH

#1738 THEIR LITTLE COWGIRL—Myrna Mackenzie
In a Fairy Tale World...
How can plain-Jane Jackie Hammond be the biological mother
of sexy rancher Stephen Collins's adorable daughter when
she's never even met him? Ask the fertility clinic! But before
Jackie gives up her newfound child, she might discover that her
little girl—and the one man who makes Jackie feel beautiful—
are worth fighting for.

#1739 GEORGIA GETS HER GROOM!—Carolyn Zane
The Brubaker Brides
Georgia Brubaker has her sights set on the perfect man.
But when she comes face-to-face with her childhood nemesis,
all her plans go out the window. The nerdy "Cootie Biggles"
has developed into supersmooth, 007-clone Carter Biggles-
Vanderhousen, who leaves Georgia shaken *and* stirred....

#1740 THE BILLIONAIRE'S WEDDING MASQUER-
ADE—Melissa McClone
Billionaires don't make very good farmhands! But
Elisabeth Wheeler is desperate for help, and Henry Davenport
is strong, available...and handsome. Henry might not have any
experience planting or ploughing, but he sure knows how to
make Elisabeth's pulse race!

#1741 CINDERELLA'S LUCKY TICKET—
Melissa James
When Lucy Miles tries to claim the house Ben Capriati won
in a sweepstakes drawing, he knows he should be furious. But
he just can't fight his attraction to the sweet but sassy librarian.
Can Ben convince Lucy to build a home with him forever?